DREAMING OVERSEAS

SIDDHARTH CHOUDHARY

BlueRose ONE .com
Stories Matter
New Delhi • London

BLUEROSE PUBLISHERS
India | U.K.

For permissions requests or inquiries regarding this publication, please contact:

BLUEROSE PUBLISHERS
www.BlueRoseONE.com
info@bluerosepublishers.com
+91 8882 898 898
+4407342408967

ISBN: 978-93-6452-982-2

Cover Design: Sadhna Kumari
Typesetting: Pooja Sharma

First Edition: December 2024

Author's Note

People often ask me where my motivation comes from, and my answer is always the same: discipline. It has been the cornerstone of my life, shaping not just my achievements but also how I have faced challenges and grown through them. While I've had the privilege of competing in national-level skating and squash championships, my biggest leap of faith came when I moved to Australia to pursue my Masters in International Relations at Monash University. Like many Indian students, I was excited about the opportunities that the foreign education promised, but I was also unprepared for the challenges that came with it. Studying abroad is far from the glossy dream we often imagine. It meant adjusting to a new culture, balancing financial pressures, navigating academic expectations, and building a life from scratch in a foreign country.

There were moments of doubt, homesickness, and frustration, but those experiences helped me grow and discover my inner strength. Through it all, I remained committed to my passions—academics, personal growth, and communication. Today, I use my platform @sidspeakofficial, to share my journey, lessons, and insights with over 130,000 followers on Instagram. As a content creator and motivational speaker, I've found purpose in inspiring others to overcome their own challenges and pursue their dreams with confidence.

I wrote 'Dreaming Overseas' to shed light on the realities of studying abroad—the highs, the lows, and the lessons that often go unspoken. My hope is that this book will guide and inspire anyone thinking of taking that step, helping them prepare for what lies ahead and embrace the transformative journey of living and learning in a new country. To all the dreamers out there: believe in yourself, stay disciplined, and keep going. The path may not be easy, but it will always be worth it.

Acknowledgments

Writing this book has been a journey of reflection and gratitude, and there are a few people without whom this wouldn't have been possible.

First and foremost, I want to thank my mother. You have always pushed me to step outside my comfort zone and explore new boundaries, teaching me to never settle for less than my best. Your unwavering belief in my abilities has been my greatest source of strength.

To my father, my rock and the foundation of my success—you've shown me the value of hard work, integrity, and resilience. Your quiet support and wisdom have guided me through the toughest of times, and I can never thank you enough for being the anchor that kept me steady.

To my younger brother, my eternal source of positivity—you've always been the light that brightens my darkest days. Your energy, optimism, and constant encouragement have been a reminder to keep moving forward no matter what.

Lastly, I want to thank every person who has been part of my journey—friends, mentors, and my incredible audience on **@sidspeakofficial**. Your support inspires me to share my story and strive for more.

This book is dedicated to all of you. Thank you for believing in me and being part of this adventure.

Introduction

Social media is swarmed with posts of Indian diaspora students showing lifestyle upgrade after moving abroad. Pictures are often taken in clubs, tourist destinations, and with newfound multicultural friend groups with honorary mentions to famous streets and lush restaurants while dressed in crisp and snazzy fits.

On the flip side, family group chats are flooded with snaps of relatives with backdrops of the London Eye, the Eiffel Tower, The Statue of Liberty, scenic beaches of Australia, and many more cliche tourist spots.

The pictures act as a window giving us a rose-tinted view of life abroad, adorned with cleaner roads, exotic cuisines, and spectacular infrastructure with an almost utopian - looking cityscape, which is in stark contrast to our immediate environment.

The idea of foreign countries embedded in many Indian's minds is the one that promises a better life, extraordinary educational and career opportunities, and a more respectable and contemporary lifestyle.

The pictures serve as a portal to a better life, the sole route through the portal in many Indian youths' minds is securing the means to study abroad.

The education system is considered metaphorical of the above euphemism, abroad education looks promising in terms of better and more flexible programs, abundant resources with a seemingly alluring cultural shift, a liberal one.

India is a relatively new sovereign state, gaining independence more than half a century ago. Post-colonization saw a tremendous cultural shift with the integration of philosophies and the overall development of a new culture and society altogether. This called for a universal approach in education if the Indian workforce were to assimilate with the rest of the world at a global pace. A lot of migration began taking place, especially for schooling. Since the foreign education system was a structure that was older than Indian independence; it was believed to be reliable in gaining up-to-date and holistic education relevant to exponentially changing shifts in arts, technology, and innovation.

Several pioneers in Indian technological, political, and trade advancements have attained their graduate or postgraduate studies from renowned universities abroad. Mahatma Gandhi gained perspective on prejudice and discrimination only upon witnessing it firsthand during his law studies in South Africa, reinforcing the impact education abroad had on shaping our country as we know it today.

The allure goes beyond the credentials and the quality of education one receives when moving to a different country to study. The lifestyle and culture also play a huge role in the interest. Growing up many Indians are exposed to various cultures through diverse media, this adds to the innate and primal curiosity to explore beyond comfort and familiarity. At a time and age when humans can interact and explore each other's diverse cultures and lifestyles, an education abroad is probably the easiest way youth can access other cultures and live amongst them.

India is a country that places an insurmountable importance on education culturally. In urban settings, an abroad degree or career is usually considered a remarkable milestone. From their very childhood, Indians are conditioned to prioritize education above many other aspects of life; it is seen as an assured way to financial and social security. In the present-day, a degree abroad is considered a massive perk; it builds you up in the social hierarchy and even helps secure nuptial bonds in some cases. It is considered the pinnacle of one's educational and career path, promising a better, happier, and wealthier life.

As the saying goes, "The grass is greener on the other side," however, a contemporary rendition adds, "But the water bills are probably higher too!" the same could be said about the infallible dream of studying overseas. The efforts taken to get to the college are more than often just the tip of the iceberg, harboring more nuances that only a person who has been through the experience can know.

This book is the story of one such idealist, called Swapnil. Swapnil's life unfolds in a very peculiar path once he sets out to fulfill his dreams of studying abroad. In navigating the troughs and crests of his new reality, he also experiences colossal growth as an individual. The journey takes one through several moments of introspection and challenges rigid beliefs while also simultaneously broadening the scope of one's perspective.

Swapnil is accompanied in his journey towards attaining his ambitions by a few distinct people he happens to befriend along the way, as well as those who have been with him long before his journey began. This read is meant to be insightful and happens to be inspiring on various notes.

Contents

Chapter 1

The Odyssey of Choice

Gentle rays of the sun caressed Swapnil's face, peeping through the little gap between the curtain and the end of the window as he lay aloof on his sturdy old chair. He looked around his dorm room, gazing at his worn textbooks stacked haphazardly on the desk, the faded posters clinging to the walls, and the old, creaky bed that had seen him through many sleepless nights. It was hard to imagine he would part ways with his familiar surroundings; the tattered remnants of the room gave him solace when times were not easy.

Swapnil is enveloped in nostalgia and ponders his time at Delhi University. He is reminded of the times when he was a young teenager stepping foot on this huge campus, an enthusiastic young boy ready to give his college life the best shot, full of aspirations and hope. He chuckles slightly, reminiscing about his days as a freshman, the feeling of newfound freedom, hope for a home away from home, and budding friendships. Late-night assignment completion or study sessions meant gatherings with his friends, indulging in multiple packets of Maggi, immersed in pockets of gossip, banter, and copious amounts of instant coffee.

However, it wasn't all fun and frolic. Swapnil thought of the times he had to give up his sleep and time due to the immense workload that demanded his utmost attention. He wasn't just going to wrap it up for the sake of it. You could say he had a streak of perfectionism in him. He wanted to present his best in whatever avenues he took up. He was determined to push himself for better results. He felt the pressure to perform, owing to gratitude for his family, but most importantly, it was the pressure that he had put on himself. He never had small aspirations; dreams were larger than life, and he wanted to turn them all into reality someday.

Despite his resolve, often he found himself faltering when it came to believing in his decisions. He wasn't sure if he had made the right choice pursuing the course he had taken up at his university. He did not know if this would lead him to his dream life. Delhi University had become a second home to him. He had grown immensely through his college journey, not just academically, but personally. He had learned to navigate the complexities of life, deal with setbacks, and push through even when the odds seemed stacked against him.

This was Swapnil's final year in college. Swapnil paced around the room restlessly. He knew he had to make a choice soon; his graduation was imminent, and he wasn't sure about what he would do next. 'Should I get a job like Papa always wanted, or should I study further?' He thought to himself. However, deep down, he already knew the answer. A job immediately after his bachelor's wasn't going to suffice for him. He wasn't even sure about the subject he was graduating in. He knew he wanted more but didn't know what 'more' meant. Swapnil's eyes restlessly wandered around the room; he fidgeted with the pages of his book, hoping some resolve would wash over him. This took him back to the time when he had finished his 12th grade and was faced with the paralyzing decision of choosing a major and his alma mater, which supposedly determined his career path for the rest of his life. The familiar dread of decision-making overwhelmed him. Even after several years at Delhi University, Swapnil felt like he had yet to gain clarity on what he truly wanted to pursue.

Swapnil laid down on his bed, lost in thoughts, he watched the fan on his ceiling whir at a monotonous and steady, yet, fast pace, symbolic of his thoughts, scurrying in a loop with no end or beginning. He opens his social media and starts scrolling through his feed, a post of a savvy-looking boy dressed up to the nines with the backdrop of a swanky club pops up, the location tagged above his post says "Melbourne, Australia", Swapnil smiles looking at the picture of his longtime friend Jaiveer.

Jaiveer and Swapnil went long back, Jaiveer was Swapnil's childhood friend, and both of them studied in the same school together, though they were very different from one another, their bond was impeccable. Jaiveer was seemingly living his best life in Melbourne, his opulent social media was a testimony to that, Swapnil found his posts to be awe-inspiring and often found himself wondering what life abroad is like. Jaiveer's message pops up on his notifications, "Hey bro, what's up?" "It's been a long time", Swapnil lights up on seeing a notification from his good friend, "I've been good Jai, just a lot of things on my mind right now" replies Swapnil. He continues to scroll through his feed and a video call notification buzzes on his phone, a call from Jaiveer. Swapnil swiftly sits upright and picks up the call.

The video call connected, and on the other side of Swapnil's screen was Jaiveer. Swapnil noticed quite a bit of change in his old friend, from the way he groomed himself to his accent; he looked like a better version of the Jaiveer he previously knew. Yet, there was a familiar warmth and comfort in his company.

Jaiveer looked at Swapnil, and his eyes lit up. "Hey, man, how has it been?" He asked with a huge grin.

Swapnil reciprocated Jaiveer's happiness upon seeing him after a long time. "I've been good, Jai. Seems like you remembered you had a friend back in Delhi today," he retorted with a mischievous laugh.

Jaiveer beamed, knowing Swapnil was the same witty boy he knew from his childhood. "I never forgot, bro. I have been meaning to talk to you for a while now. I saw your text and thought I'd catch up with you real quick," he mentioned. "You said something about having a lot on your mind. You good, Swapnil?" Asked Jaiveer with a concerned tone.

Swapnil chuckled nervously, "I'm glad you decided to call. I wanted to talk to you about this," he replied.

"Sure, man. I'm here for you always," said Jaiveer reassuringly.

"I've been thinking a lot about my future lately, and I could really use your advice," said Swapnil.

"What's been on your mind? Tell me everything," enquired Jaiveer.

"It's my last year at college. I'm not sure what comes after. Papa says getting a job should be my next priority, but I know there is more for me to do, you know? I want something bigger, Jai, something like you have going on for yourself. You seem so sorted; I admire that about you. I believe going abroad for my master's would be the right thing to do, but I'm not sure, given my circumstances and parents' expectations. It's just that I have so many things I want to do and be, but my head is so clouded lately, I'm stuck in this no man's land between my own aspirations and expectations and those of my family and society."

A quiet moment engulfed the FaceTime call after Swapnil poured his heart out to Jaiveer. Jaiveer absorbed everything Swapnil shared with him. He was mildly surprised to hear that Swapnil thought he had a perfect life, but he quickly composed himself and endeavored to reassure his perplexed friend.

"I understand where you're coming from bro," Jaiveer said. "It's natural to feel torn between different options, especially when there's so much uncertainty about the future. But you have to trust yourself, trust your instincts, and follow your heart. That's the only way you'll find true happiness and fulfillment," Jaiveer exclaimed. The words resonated deeply with him; maybe taking his own advice would benefit him, he thought.

Swapnil felt a wave of relief wash over him. All he sought from Jai was his reassurance and heartfelt advice. Unbeknownst to him, Jaiveer had provided some reassurance to himself as well. . "Thanks, Jai, I really needed to hear that. I believe the best choice stems from our intuition," Swapnil shared.

"Absolutely. Feel free to reach out to me anytime, Swapnil. I'm always here for you," Jaiveer insisted.

Swapnil let out a comforted sigh, "I'll see you soon, Jai, and likewise, I'm here for you too," expressed Swapnil.

"I'll look forward to seeing you then. Bye, buddy, take care," Jaiveer bid his farewell, ending the call.

Swapnil took a deep breath of relief. He had an idea of what he wanted to do, but having the idea validated by one of his closest friends and someone he looked up to reinforced his belief further. He felt determined to pursue his dreams of studying abroad after his heartfelt conversation with Jaiveer.

He pulled out his computer and started looking up courses and colleges to study abroad; he was staggered by the sheer amount of options presented to him, submerging him into the paradox of choice. He was more frazzled as time went by; He decided to step out for a breather. He sighed out loud and gently leaned against a wall, gazing at the horizon. The endless horizon between the deep orange sky with a setting sun and a skyline ignited him to wonder about his own future, not bound by anyone else but him and his choices. A multitude of thoughts came running to his head, some of self-doubt, some of ambition. He dreamt of a life filled with comfort and purpose, one that fulfilled him thoroughly, akin to the Japanese concept of ikigai. Swapnil was determined to be able to fulfill his goal of studying abroad, he knew it would take an immense amount of effort, but he knew if he persisted he would be able to achieve what he wanted. However, Swapnil felt he didn't have enough resources or connections to be able to navigate this journey by himself, so he decided to get help from a consultancy.

Swapnil woke up earlier than usual the next day and headed to his class beaming with joy. He had scheduled a consultation with the agency later that evening, and throughout the class, he kept fantasizing about the kind of life he would have abroad, the places he would get to travel, the food he would get to try and the friends he would make. He turned the pages of his notes mindlessly, lost in rampant imagination. And yet, he had a recurring thought at the back of his mind, one that got him worried about how he would break this news to his family, especially his father. “I just hope Papa understands where I’m coming from.” He thinks to himself. He gathers all his things and packs up to leave the class, deciding to head straight to the study abroad agency.

He nervously enters the consultation building. He peers around the waiting room sheepishly, looking at the framed testimonials of students who pursued their education abroad with the help of the agency. Their testimonials echoed the classic narrative of a study abroad success story.

Upon looking at the frames, he feels assured about his choice. With a set of notes containing questions he has for the counselor, he makes his way into the cabin of the counselor. On opening the door, he is greeted by a polite elderly woman; the lines across her forehead and eyes acted as a testament to her years of wisdom. Swapnil greets her with a warm smile and settles into his seat. "So tell me, Swapnil, how can we help you today?" The counselor greets with a fond smile.

"I have been wanting to explore my study abroad options, but I'm unsure how to go about it. I don't have much clarity regarding the subject I want to study either." He shared.

"That's more common that you'd think" she laughed. "Given your aspirations and dreams I'm sure we can figure something out, you seem like a determined kid," she remarked.

The counselor's statement got Swapnil's spirits up, "thank you! I would love to talk more about the opportunities I could explore and the ways to go about the application procedure," said Swapnil.

"From finance to MBA, from technology to Economics, you have a myriad of doors open for you Swapnil, all you have to do is figure out what aligns best with your interest and long term goals and we could hash out a plan accordingly," replied the counselor.

Swapnil elaborated on his goals and strengths in an attempt to narrow down a couple of options. The counselor listened to him attentively, trying to ease his worries and clarify his doubts. Throughout the meeting, Swapnil gained substantial insight into the whole process of applying to colleges abroad and how the education system is different from the one he was familiar with. The conversation with the counselor further strengthened his resolve of getting into a college abroad for his masters.

Swapnil thanked the counselor for her time and took his leave, he walked out of the building feeling different, and he now had a strong purpose to work towards. "I have a really good feeling about this, all that is left to do is share my plans with papa and ma," Swapnil reflected. He excitedly texted Jai about the new developments on his plan, his meeting with the agency counselor and her insights. While walking back his phone beeped with a notification from Jaiveer, it read "I believe in you bro, you have my best wishes." Swapnil felt a wave of gratitude gush over him, Jaiveer's support overwhelmed him.

Swapnil recollected memories from his past, of when he was a child and dreamt of moving abroad and building a career overseas, making his family proud. He felt closer to the dream as each day passed by; he wondered what the future had in store for him.

Chapter 2

A New Horizon

Swapnil treaded on the familiar path to home that evoked strong feelings within him. On the way, his mind began spiraling. He thought of the many ways that the discussion would unfold if he entrusted his father with his aspiration. Given the circumstances at his home, he was troubled by the thought of his father deeming he was way too ambitious for his own good. He was not too sure about how he would actualize his dreams once his father approved of his decision to study abroad either, most of the time he was a self-assured young man, however, when stakes involved finances and other loops that intersected with different facets of his life like his family, he was bound to think about it for longer. He was riddled with doubts and needed desperate assurance from his father, a man he really looked up to.

Swapnil rang the bell of his home, heaving a sigh of anticipation. The door opened and he sees his mother, radiant as ever, she welcomes him with a gleaming smile and gives him a tight hug.

"Ma please, I just got home let me breathe first," he laughed.

Swapnil's mother was elated to see her son after a long time, "come in, papa is waiting for you! He bought your favourite sweets for you to eat," she said, with her eyes welling up.

Swapnil felt a surge of warmth take over his body, he had missed his family. He walked inside and saw his father sitting up on the sofa; he looked like he had been expecting Swapnil's arrival. "How have you been, beta? Have you been taking care of yourself?" Asked Swapnil's father with a tender and protective tone.

"I have been great papa, I scored well this semester, I'm just hoping to keep it up next semester as well" he replied, hoping his father would be happy to hear the news.

"I'm proud of you, beta. I know you'll go a long way, just remain steadfast and keep moving on the right path," Swapnil's father expressed.

Swapnil did not know how to interpret the statement his father had just uttered: 'What is the right path? Is going abroad for my education a right choice? Knowing it would financially strain my family if I left for education abroad instead of finding a job after my graduation and supporting them, am I making a selfish choice or would it be a worthy investment?' He wondered to himself.

He smiled softly and responded to his father, "Thank you, Papa, I'm hoping for the best."

Swapnil found himself getting cozy in his old room, he missed his bed, and it was old but felt like a warm embrace. He lay down and snuggled towards his side, thinking of his childhood at his home.

He remembered an incident from when he was a little boy, just about ten years old. He had an elocution or a speaking contest at his school the next day, his mother helped him memorize his lines while he was trepid with sweat purging out of his palms. "Ma I don't want to participate in the competition tomorrow, I'm not prepared," he wailed. "Swapnil you cannot give up at the last moment, you have prepared enough to participate, don't give me excuses," retorted his mother sternly.

Swapnil ended up throwing a tantrum, refusing to practice his lines and sobbing loudly. His father overheard the ordeal and approached him.

“I want you to stop crying firstly, now tell me beta, what is bothering you so much? I know it is not about your lack of preparation, you were so excited just a few days ago” cited his father, keenly.

“Papa I just don't feel like participating, I know everyone else will be better than I am and I will end up losing,” whined little Swapnil.

“So that is what this is about then, are you afraid of losing?” Asked his father.

“I don't want to participate if I won't win a prize, what is the point then?” retorted Swapnil.

“Well, the point is to go beyond your comfort zone, take up new challenges, and learn from your experiences.” Swapnil’s father claimed.

Young Swapnil was confused and found no weight in his father's words; he gazed at his father's serene yet unrelenting face, wondering what he had meant by that. However, he did end up having to participate owing to his mother's burgeoning temper, little Swapnil knew better than to go against his mother's words. To his surprise, as far as he remembered, he had performed quite well and had ended up receiving the first place. Swapnil reflected on this incident, thinking of all the times his father encouraged him to push his limits and to keep trying new things. He speculated if he had inherited his risk-taking streak from his father. Looking back he realized his father never barred him from doing things differently, exploring, and messing up, in fact, he prodded Swapnil to push the limits of his potential.

He reminisced on the fond memories with his family, knowing that he always had them no matter what. Swapnil drifted into a deep slumber with a content mind, he felt the buzzing in his mind cease, and he knew exactly what he had to do next.

The next day morning, Swapnil woke up feeling revitalized after a much-needed night's sleep in his old room. He sat across from his father at the dining table for breakfast; he guzzled down his mother's home cooked paratha that he desperately craved when he had to eat the bland, repetitive mess food at his college. After devouring his scrumptious breakfast, Swapnil gathered the courage to talk to his family about his newfound aspiration. "Papa, I wanted to talk to you about something, it's really important," exclaimed Swapnil.

"Sure beta, go ahead," replied his father.

"I know of your expectations, I'm aware that you would appreciate me getting a job and starting my career after my graduation, but I have been thinking about it for a while now and I have made a different choice." Swapnil confided.

Swapnil's father was taken aback upon hearing his son's confession; he remained still for what seemed like an eternity to Swapnil. He put on his glasses and gathered his eyebrows towards his eyes, a face he made when serious about something.

"Tell me more, I'm listening," replied Swapnil's father.

"I want to go abroad to pursue my master's, I have thought about this, and I'm sure about my decision." Swapnil professed.

"That is quite unexpected, when did you decide on this?" Retorted his father.

"I understand, Dad. But the opportunities abroad are immense. The exposure, and the quality of education could change everything for me. I have been wanting to pursue my masters abroad for quite some time now, but a conversation with Jaiveer, my friend, cemented my decision," he relented.

“I've even looked into education loans.” Swapnil added quickly, hoping to preempt his father's financial concerns.

His father sat silently for a moment, absorbing the information. Finally, he spoke. "Swapnil, I have always wanted the best for you. If this is something you truly believe in, we will find a way. Let’s discuss this further and see how we can make it happen."

Encouraged by his father’s openness, Swapnil shared more details about his research and the potential benefits of studying abroad. His father listened intently, nodding occasionally. The conversation stretched for hours, covering everything from financial logistics to the emotional challenges of studying in a foreign country. Swapnil felt the confidence in him surge as he spoke to his father, with every nod of approval, A keen and intent expression on his father's face, he grew more vary of the fact that his father was open to him trying out this life-altering experience.

Swapnil’s father was aware of the laurels that one could gain if they secured an education abroad, it was even better if they managed to secure a career abroad. He knew his son's immense potential and was eminently proud of him for taking a stand deep down.

“Swapnil, I'll be honest, you have fully convinced me, it looks like you have done your fair share of research beta,” spoke Swapnil's father.

"I had to, I truly want to do this papa," replied Swapnil.

His father let out a proud grin and hugged him.

"You'll do really well, I'm sure of that, you should proceed with the applications and initiate the process Swapnil, time is key here," he proclaimed with a stern tone.

"I'll schedule a meeting with the bank to explore the possibility of an education loan," offered his father.

"Thank you for supporting me through this papa, it means a lot." Swapnil replies in gratitude.

His father pulls him in for an embrace, hiding his teary-eyed proud face.

Swapnil is left feeling confident and gains a tremendous amount of clarity after the conversation with his father. His mother rejoiced after being told of the decision and gave Swapnil her heartfelt blessings to move forward with his plan.

Swapnil walks towards the bank, accompanied by his father, armed with his documents and credentials in a file that he clutches onto with his right hand. Both enter the bank building and head towards the loan consultant. As they wait in the bank's lobby, Swapnil feels a mix of nerves and excitement. The bank officer, a stern-looking man in his fifties, invites them into his office asks them to explain their situation.

Swapnil's father spoke of his son's aspiration to pursue his postgrad abroad, he highlighted that their present financial condition was not conducive to fully finance Swapnil's education abroad.

On hearing this Swapnil felt a pang of guilt hit him, he felt a sense of overbearing responsibility come over him.

The conversation between Swapnil's father and the bank officer treaded between configuring the expenses to going through the paperwork to verify credentials.

"The plan sounds decent, do you have a collateral to secure the loan?" Asked the bank officer.

"Yes, me and my wife have decided to offer our house as the collateral," Swapnil's father stated.

Swapnil, who was listening to his father intently, was taken aback by the new revelation. The gravity of his situation dawned upon him.

"Great, all that's left to do is for you to submit paper work and we'll evaluate them and get back to you, we can start the official loan application as soon as everything checks out," proclaimed the officer.

"Well keep in touch, thank you for your time," Swapnil's father extended his gratitude towards the officer, shook his hand, and parted. Swapnil could hardly contain his excitement. However, he was now starkly aware of the commitment he had to fulfil, he was also immensely grateful for his father's unwavering support and sacrifice.

"Well, that's one hurdle down, lot more to go before you get to where you want to be young man," chuckled his father.

Swapnil smiled at his father and thanked him for his support in inciting the beginning of his journey.

Swapnil left the bank a happy man, awaiting his appointment with the study abroad consultancy to hash out the rest of the process.

He reached the consultancy and was greeted warmly by the same counselor he had consulted with during his first meeting. He smiled at her, "I'm back this time with my documents, hopefully, we can start working on my applications!" he said.

The counselor laughed, "Of course sir, that's what I'm here for, I'm glad you decided to stick with your decision," she affirmed.

He submitted everything required to initiate the admission process. The agency's counselor was supportive and efficient, guiding him through each step with precision.

One of the crucial requirements was taking the IELTS exam, an English proficiency test necessary for admission to most universities abroad. The test evaluated basic speaking and writing skills, with the highest possible score being nine bands. As a student at Delhi University, Swapnil felt confident in his command of the English language, but he knew preparation was key.

The weeks leading up to the exam were intense. Swapnil juggled his university coursework with rigorous IELTS preparation. He enrolled in a preparatory course, attended practice sessions, and took countless mock tests. His evenings were spent poring over vocabulary lists and grammar exercises, while his weekends were dedicated to honing his speaking skills through conversations with friends and language partners.

Despite the grueling schedule, Swapnil felt a sense of fulfillment. Each day brought him closer to his dream. The support from his family and friends fueled his determination, and he found himself embracing the challenge with renewed vigor.

The night before the IELTS exam, Swapnil sat at his desk, flipping through the pages of the exam booklet he had picked up during his preparation course. As he skimmed through the sections, a sense of ease washed over him. The questions seemed straightforward, and the tasks manageable. Confident in his English skills, he found it hard to muster any nerves. The months of rigorous preparation had made him feel ready, perhaps even over-prepared, for what lay ahead.

The next morning, Swapnil arrived at the test center well ahead of time. The scene that greeted him was quite different from what he had imagined. Clusters of students stood in the courtyard, their faces etched with anxiety. Parents huddled close, offering whispered prayers and blessings. The atmosphere was charged with a palpable tension, a stark contrast to Swapnil's calm demeanor.

As he watched a particularly intense group of students frantically flipping through their notes, Swapnil felt a twinge of curiosity. Approaching a student who appeared especially stressed, he asked a question.

"Hey, is this your first time taking the test?" Swapnil asked, trying to sound casual.

The student, a young man with tired eyes, looked up and sighed. "No, this is my third attempt. I've already failed twice. It's really difficult, man." He complained.

Swapnil was taken aback. "Really? I thought the test was pretty basic. The practice materials didn't seem too bad." Swapnil replied.

The student gave him a wry smile. "Maybe for you, but for many of us, it's a huge challenge. My future depends on this score. Without it, I can't get into the university I want." He chided.

Swapnil's confidence wavered. Had he underestimated the exam? The gravity of the situation began to dawn on him. For many, this test was not just a stepping stone but a significant hurdle.

As the test began, Swapnil settled into his seat. The listening section started, and he focused intently on the recordings. To his surprise, the questions were as straightforward as he had expected. The reading passages, too, were clear and comprehensible. By the time he reached the writing section, his initial anxiety had faded, replaced by a sense of familiarity and ease. He crafted his essay and interpreted the graph with confidence, drawing on his academic background. Finally, it was time for the speaking test. Swapnil entered the examination room, greeted the examiner, and answered the questions with clarity and poise. The scenarios presented were manageable, and he navigated through them with ease. As the test concluded, Swapnil felt a mixture of relief and confusion. The exam had been exactly as he had anticipated, basic and nominal.

Exiting the test center, Swapnil observed the other test-takers. Many were visibly distressed, some wiping away tears, others discussing the difficulty of the questions. Conversations buzzed around him, filled with expressions of doubt and worry.

"I don't know if I'll pass this time." A student lamented to her friend.

"I blanked out during the listening section again," another admitted, his voice tinged with frustration.

Swapnil stood there, witnessing the scene. It was the first time he truly understood the disparity in experiences. His own exposure, education, and preparation had given him a sense of confidence that many of his peers lacked. For him, the test was a procedural step; for others, it was a formidable barrier. On his ride back home, Swapnil pondered over the day's events. He realized how fortunate he was to have had the resources and support that made the exam seem less daunting. It wasn't just about academic preparation; it was about the broader context—educational background, access to resources, and emotional support.

Chapter 3

A New Beginning

At the brink of sundown, Swapnil settled into his study table with a warm mug of coffee by his side. He had a rigorous lecture earlier that afternoon, he was at the end of his third year, and a studious atmosphere engulfed the college. With the semester exams drawing closer every day, Students formed group study sessions, and spent the dawn at libraries instead of sleeping till class. His batchmates especially, were in the same boat as he was. Some knew their path, while the others scrambled from one class to another just trying to get by, uncertain of what they intended on doing next.

Swapnil turns pages of his study material keenly, trying to get a hold of the vast syllabus before him. He knew the first step toward putting his plans into action was by excelling academically. A great academic record could open up vast choices and avenues for his future.

He already had his eyes set on a college abroad; he knew every nook and corner of the campus by the number of videos he had watched about it, the courses, the faculty, and the student life. He thought he had it all figured out.

He was immersed in books when he was not busy scramming to lectures and following up with his abroad education consultancy. It was a rigorous period, and he barely had time to indulge in any other activities, he kept telling himself "When all this is figured out I'll have plenty of time to myself" he firmly believed that his hard work would pay off and translate into a rewarding experience.

He kept reminding himself of how far he had come, from not being sure of what he wanted to do next, to being in the process of securing a seat at a university abroad.

Most importantly, he had his entire family rooting for him amidst unsolicited advice from relatives and other people who did not see his vision or potential.

His education consultant applied to various masters programs for him, each application a leap of faith, he was constantly in touch with them, updating them and receiving updates from them. The consultancy proved to be very beneficial to him due to his hectic schedule, they eased the seemingly daunting process of applying to colleges abroad.

One afternoon, he called his education consultant to catch up on updates concerning his application to his dream university, the phone rang and his consultant picked up on the other side.

"Hello, I wanted to know the status of my application to the university I mentioned I was keen on joining, any updates on it yet?" He asked anticipatingly.

"Hello Swapnil, I'm afraid we might not have great news for you, your application did not meet the university course requirements, I'm pretty sure you must have received a mail confirming the same," replied the consultant.

Swapnil could not comprehend what he had just heard, he was in disbelief. He thanked the consultant for her update and hung up the call.

He immediately opened his email and looked for the mail amongst a bunch of spam mail.

"Ugh, about time I clear my email," he sighed to himself. Upon scrolling for a while he came across a mail from the university and eagerly opened it.

The mail confirmed his worst fears; his application was rejected due to unfulfilled criteria's in his application.

The rejection took a tremendous toll on Swapnil, he was unable to focus on anything else, he knew there were a lot of other opportunities awaiting him, but he wasn't sure if they were as good as the university he had his eyes on. He grappled with low self-esteem for a while.

When he got on a call with his mother, she could tell something was off. "Anything wrong beta? You seem upset about something."

Swapnil replied, confiding in his mother about his rejection from his dream university.

His mother listened keenly and offered him solace through her words, "It is a part and parcel of life, don't hold on to something that was never meant for you in the first place, see this as a redirection and not a rejection Swapnil." She asserted.

Her words felt like the warmth from a bonfire on the coldest day of winter. He was upset about the rejection, but he decided not to let it weigh him down anymore, he nudged the educational consultancy to keep applying to colleges and update him regularly.

Amid this disappointment, The educational consultant called Swapnil in for a session.

"Hi Swapnil, how are you doing?" She asked him.

"I'm doing fine, just stressed about the status of applications," he replied with a mellow tone.

"Well we're here to talk about just that, I went through your application again, and upon a thorough review, I think your application could be a good match for a different course. It's a new and upcoming branch that has an exceeding potential, I want you to give a thought about it," she stated.

"Umm, sure, what course are you referring to though?" Questioned Swapnil.

"I'm talking about data science, Swapnil." The educational consultant replied.

Swapnil did not expect that, "I've heard of it but I barely know anything about it, I'll need to look into it and get back to you," he retorted.

He began researching and studying the scope of the subject and was pleasantly surprised at the scope it offered. Initially, this was not part of his plan. However, the course came with significant advantages. He called up his educational consultant and prompted her to go forward with the applications for the course.

On a seemingly uneventful day, an unexpected opportunity presented itself. He received the news that he was offered admission to a related course in data science. Swapnil couldn't believe his eyes, he re-read the email quite a few times before it hit him. He rejoiced over the admission offer, it was from a reputable college. However, he needed to figure out the course he was offered admission to.

Data science was a rapidly growing field with substantial career prospects, especially in Australia. The course promised job opportunities and the potential for permanent residency, as data science was listed on Australia's State Occupation List (SOL). Australia's State Occupation List plays a crucial role in the country's skilled migration program, particularly for students and professionals who are planning their academic or career pathways. Each state and territory in Australia maintains its own State Occupation List, which outlines the occupations that are in demand within that specific region. These lists are part of the broader Skilled Migration Program, where states and territories nominate individuals for skilled visas based on the occupations they need.

Though he had reservations, Swapnil weighed the pros and cons. The promise of job opportunities and potential permanent residency in Australia outweighed his initial hesitation. He did, after all, appreciate the scope of being able to acquire residency abroad, he was eclectic just imagining how his life would turn out if he did indeed end up settling down in Melbourne. He wouldn't be the one gaping in awe when he saw his friends abroad posting their lavish lifestyles and newfound freedom, he would be on the other side of the screen, living out his best life, the same way his friend Jaiveer was.

He was eager to take up the opportunity, he had a strong gut feeling about it. Convincing his family was a crucial step, he was well aware that they would take a while to acclimate to yet another shift, the course was not a part of the initial plan Swapnil had presented to his parents.

He had to convince them, he had to back himself with a well-researched case, highlighting the long-term benefits of the course and the opportunities it could provide.

He blew the lid on the new development to his parents. They were concerned about the deviation from his original plan. His father especially, did not like fleeting plans, given how big of a decision it was.

"Are you sure about this? This change is so drastic Swapnil, will you be able to manage the coursework?" His father uttered.

"I have studied and researched all there is to know about the course and the scope it has to offer papa, it was a well-informed decision, I think it would be a huge benefit to my career if I go ahead with it," Swapnil claimed.

"If you're firm on your stance we truly have nothing much to say, it must be something if you insist it is," his father surmised. His family was eventually persuaded by Swapnil's determination and the promising prospects. His belief in himself was the driving factor for them to encourage him to go ahead with the decision. After much contemplation and discussions with his family, friends, and mentors, Swapnil decided to pursue the data science course.

The first person who he thought of sharing the news with was Jaiveer. He enthusiastically called him up to share the news with him.

"Hey man, how have you been since the last time we spoke?" Swapnil asked

"I have been good bro, the same old. You tell me, what have you been doing," he let out a feeble chuckle.

"Well that's great, I wanted to let you know that I got into a university in Melbourne, Australia. I've been offered a seat in data science, I know it was not my initial plan, but I'm so stoked man!" He exclaimed.

"Damn, that's really something Swapnil! Look at you go, man, you're so close to coming here," replied a surprised Jaiveer.

"I know right! Can't wait to get there and live the life of my dreams, it looks so fun out there, must be nice having all the freedom and exploring life," Swapnil said gleamingly.

Jaiveer laughed, "well don't get your hopes too high, it's the same anywhere you go, it's just a change in lifestyle," Jaiveer replied.

Swapnil was surprised to hear Jaiveer say that, he chose to ignore Jaiveer's statement. "Well, I'll only know when I'm there and I have a great feeling about it," he retorted.

"Of course, bro, I'll be waiting for you! Hope to see you soon man, would be nice to catch up after so long," Jaiveer said, earnestly.

"I'll keep you updated Jai, I have to get back to studying now, I'll talk to you later," added Swapnil.

"Sure, take care." Jaiveer bid his adieu and cut the call.

Talking to Jaiveer was a pleasant break, though he pondered over why he would say that it would be the same anywhere in the world, he was keen on knowing what Jaiveer meant by that. Knowing Jaiveer, he knew he was sensible and always served Swapnil the cold hard truth even when he did not want to hear it, Swapnil decided to redirect his focus toward his exam preparation.

Swapnil swept through his preparation effortlessly, he had begun his preparation long back. He wanted to do his best and clear the exams with flying colors, day in and out he was laser-focused on getting all the syllabus covered thoroughly, The college offer in hand propelled him towards giving his best in the exams.

The exams passed like a breeze, they were over before he knew it. With his final year exams over and results pending, Swapnil received a conditional offer from the university in Australia. This offer would become unconditional once he submitted his final exam results. Confident in his academic performance, Swapnil quickly shifted his focus to the next steps: securing a visa and preparing for his journey.

Applying for a student visa can be a daunting process, often fraught with bureaucratic hurdles and long waiting periods. Swapnil anxiously applied for his visa, expecting it to take quite a bit of time to get approved. However, to his pleasant surprise, Swapnil's application was approved in a mere three minutes, a stroke of luck that further fueled his excitement. He was baffled at his luck and was overjoyed. He felt it was a sign that it was meant to be, with everything going in his favor, he was elated. On days when he had nothing to do, he would start looking up Melbourne, Australia, and his college. He loved planning what he could do, the paces he would visit, and the people he would meet once he got there.

He celebrated the end of his exams and the Visa approval by going out with his friends after a long time. He had missed spending time with his peers. However, he knew it could not be helped because of the amount of pressure he was under. He had his priorities in place. He and his friends celebrated the end of their glorious three years at Delhi University to the fullest extent, parties were being thrown far and wide, movie marathons were in and books were forgotten all too quickly. They rejoiced and indulged in fun from sunrise to sundown.

Swapnil sighed, knowing all this would come to an end as he now had to embark on a different journey, he reminisced all the times he spent together with his friends, the memories they shared, his cramped dorm which felt like an abode after a long day of classes, he was sure to cherish these memories for the rest of his life.

With the visa secured, he immersed himself in preparations for his move to Australia.

Chapter 4

The Farewell

Swapnil made his way out of the educational consultancy after his last meeting with them. He was fidgety with anticipation. As he paced towards his home, he recalled his meeting. He was immensely grateful and thanked the consultant from the bottom of his heart for being a key catalyst in his endeavor to study abroad. His one-way ticket to Melbourne, Australia was booked and he was on the last leg of his application process.

At home, Swapnil began planning a farewell party with plans of inviting his nearest and dearest. He scrolled through the internet and his memory to pick out the best venue, he wanted to leave Delhi with one final party that left a lasting impression. It was important to him, as he did not know the next time he would be able to see his friends. After college, they all had diverse plans for life, some staying back in India, others, like Swapnil deciding to venture overseas. Some planned to continue their studies while others started working right after their graduation.

The group chat was beginning to mellow down, the college friend groups were preoccupied with the huge shift after graduation, perhaps the farewell party would be a good excuse for one last get-together, Swapnil thought. Besides, he also wanted to acknowledge the role of his peers in him being able to secure a seat in a university abroad, from borrowing and lending notes to confiding in his friends when he was hitting a rough patch, they had been essential to his journey, even influential at particular times.

With just a month left before his departure, Swapnil chose a cozy restaurant for its intimate atmosphere, one that was within close proximity to everyone he had planned on inviting, where he could spend quality time with his friends and share laughter and sorrow.

He called up his friends, one after another, personally inviting them to his farewell party. He planned out a beautiful evening, in hope that everyone would find as much joy in the get-together as he would.

The invites were sent out RSVPs rolled in, the days leading up to the party, Swapnil was preoccupied with shopping for Melbourne and getting all his essentials sorted. He was beyond thrilled to be setting out on this venture abroad. His friends were equally enthralled and suggested to him places to visit in Melbourne, food to try out, and things to do, with all the bits of information and knowledge they had through the books, blogs, and social media.

The day of his farewell party was upon him, it felt quite personal and bittersweet, having to celebrate with his dear ones for perhaps, the last time in a long while.

Swapnil dressed to the nines on the day of his farewell party, he picked out his favorite t-shirt, layering it with a chic jacket he brought earlier as a part of the wardrobe he would be taking abroad. He gazed into the mirror while brushing his hair, taking a scoop of a hair gel and massaging it into his locks, gently styling it with his fingers intertwined in between his strands. “I don't look bad tonight,” he whispered with a smirk. He spent a good amount of time grooming himself well, spraying himself with copious amounts of his most expensive perfume before heading out to the party.

As the evening of the farewell party arrived, the restaurant started filling in with Swapnil’s friends. Swapnil was one of the first to reach the restaurant, he greeted each friend of his as they made their way into the table. Soon enough, food and drinks started pouring in.

The restaurant buzzed with laughter and the clinking of glasses. Swapnil stood up to address his friends, his voice filled with raw emotions. "I can't express how much your support has meant to me," he began. "Each one of you has played a role in getting me to this point, and I'm incredibly grateful. My dream of studying abroad is about to come true, and I hope to make you all proud." His friends cheered, clapping and raising their glasses in a toast to Swapnil's future.

The night was filled with reminiscing about old times, heartfelt conversations, and promises to stay in touch. He remembered the times when his friends took care of him when he was sick in college, from arranging his meals to helping him catch up with coursework, the friends from his college had made it seem like a home away from home.

His childhood friends, on the other hand, had witnessed Swapnil turn from a playful young boy to a young adult, striving to make the best out of his life; he appreciated their support and company throughout the time they knew one another.

The rest of the night was filled with music, laughter, and tears. Swapnil was surprised to see his friends gift him farewell presents. "You didn't have to guys, this is really sweet," he conveyed trying not to give in to his emotions.

Swapnil felt a mixture of excitement and sadness, knowing he was about to embark on a new chapter of his life while leaving behind a significant part of his past. The day ended faster than any of them would have liked it to; one after the other Swapnil's friends bid their farewell and took their leave. He acknowledged and appreciated his friends for their love and support, bidding a very emotional goodbye.

Swapnil wrapped up the celebrations and set out on his way back home.

On the way home, memories with his friends replayed in his head. He was indulged in nostalgia; it felt bittersweet leaving behind a huge part of his life to start one anew. As the cool night's breeze caressed Swapnil's face, he felt a solemn yet hopeful bearing come over him. With only a while left till he left for a long time, he was left reflecting on the life he knew so far.

Days passed swiftly as Swapnil was swept up amok navigating the paperwork, procuring essentials, and figuring out his itinerary. The days leading up to D-day passed in a blur, his family too was caught up in aiding him in his packing and preparation.

The day of his departure arrived sooner than expected. Swapnil's house was a whirlwind of activity as he made last-minute preparations. He rushed from one chore to another, weighing his bag in intervals as his mother stuffed them with snacks and edible assortments in intervals. "Ma, please stop adding food to the luggage last minute! I really do not have the time for this." Swapnil said, annoyed.

"You'll be homesick in no time without your favorite snacks and sweets, don't call me up complaining about how much you miss Indian food then," she responded.

"They have Indian food in Melbourne Ma," replied Swapnil.

His mother pouted exasperatedly, "It's your choice at the end," she said, visibly upset.

Swapnil couldn't bear to upset his mother, especially on a day like today. "I'm sorry, I'll make space for the snacks, and thank you for always thinking of my comfort," he expressed. With a warm smile on his face.

Swapnil's mother held back her tears; she was used to him being away from home for a long time for his undergrad. However, it was going to be different this time. She knew it would be quite a long time till she could see her son in person after he left today.

His parents, trying to keep their emotions in check, busied themselves with ensuring everything was in order. His bags were packed, documents double-checked, and goodbyes to neighbors and relatives said.

The car ride to the airport was a somber journey. Swapnil's parents offered him advice with a tone of concern and care. "Stay out of trouble," his father cautioned. "Focus on your studies and make the most of this opportunity," his mother added. "Avoid conflicts and take care of your health," they both urged. Tears welled up in their eyes as they spoke, their voices wavering with emotion.

Swapnil, gazing out of the window, felt a lump in his throat. He pondered over his childhood at home, the aroma of the food being cooked in the kitchen by his mother, taking over his senses every day after he got home from school, his father and him playing cricket every weekend in a park close to his home and the banters and waves of laughter that filled the dinner table after a long day. He would miss his home and family so much.

As the car drove by each landmark, Swapnil's eyes drifted from one street lamp to another, arranged in an equidistant and orderly manner. His thoughts meandered from one lamp post to the next. Delhi was close to his heart, he had been born and brought up in this city, it was where he turned into a young adult from an unassuming little boy, and it was where he had built long-lasting friendships, friendships that transcended time and distance.

He wondered how Jaiveer must have felt, leaving behind a home that he had known since his birth to a completely foreign land and starting over from scratch. "Did he feel the things I'm feeling now? Was it just as hard for him?" He thought to himself. He rolled down the car windows and let the wind brush across his face.

His parents sat in solemn silence, ruminating about their son's departure to a new place. No one uttered a word during the quiet drive to the airport, except for occasional checklists and asking the driver how long it would take to reach the airport. There was no audible exchange of words. However, a lot was being said just by their silence.

He realized just how big of a part his parents played in him getting to where he was. All the sacrifices his father had to make, all the hours he toiled at work so Swapnil could live a comfortable life. All the time his mother spent, getting young Swapnil to finish his homework, and get him prepped for his exams while managing the household and family responsibilities. He had to take over the responsibility of his family someday, he was sure to make them proud.

He envisioned the life awaiting him in Australia—a land of opportunities where his dreams could come true. As the car approached the airport, the reality of his departure began to sink in. He was leaving his comfort zone, and stepping into an unknown world.

As soon as they arrived at the airport, Swapnil and his father rushed to unload the luggage from the cab. Swapnil tries to stop his father, "It's alright papa, I got this," as he tries to pick the bag from his father's hands.

"You are on your own when you go to Melbourne, Swapnil. Let me at least help you for as long as I can," murmured his father, fighting back the tears.

Swapnil let out an emotional sigh, he nodded at what his father told and both of them carried the luggage towards the entrance.

At the airport, the atmosphere was a mix of excitement and sadness. Swapnil's friends had come to see him off, their faces reflecting a blend of pride and sorrow. As it was time to say goodbye, Swapnil embraced each of them, feeling the weight of their emotions.

"We'll miss you man, hope you won't forget us when you find new friends abroad," his friends chime in, with tears welling up in their eyes.

"Don't cry," Swapnil said, trying to lighten the mood. "I'm off to fulfill my dreams. I'll call you as soon as I land."

His friends, fighting back tears, nodded and wished him luck. His mother pulled him in for a tight embrace, "take care of yourself, eat well, and call us every day," she demanded as she sobbed uncontrollably. Swapnil's father gave his son a tight hug and his blessings, "Best of luck beta, work hard and take care of yourself," he said.

"You too papa, take care of yourself, I'll miss you and Mom a lot. See you." He replies. He quickly composes himself after a heartwarming farewell with his friends and family and starts walking towards the entrance.

With a final wave, Swapnil turned and walked towards the departure gates. He cleared immigration, his heart pounding with a mix of anxiety and anticipation. As he boarded the flight, he couldn't help but notice the other students and parents around him, all dreamers like him, embarking on similar journeys.

Swapnil boards onto his flight, walking down the aisle while looking around the seat labels, trying to ascertain his seat. He finds his seat, places his luggage in the overhead bin, and settles into his seat with his headphones on with an extensive playlist of his favorite songs downloaded for the long journey.

The 14-hour flight was a time for reflection. Swapnil took photos of the view from his window seat, capturing the sunset and the vast expanse of the sky. As the plane soared through the clouds, he felt a sense of liberation but also an overwhelming awareness of how alone he was in this new journey. The flight attendants served meals, and passengers around him chatted or slept, each lost in their own thoughts.

Swapnil used the time to think about the future. He thought about the data science course, the university, and the opportunities that awaited him.

As the plane descended and the announcement for landing was made, Swapnil felt a surge of excitement. He was about to step foot on Australian soil, a place he had only seen in pictures and heard about in stories. The moment the plane touched down, Swapnil knew his life was about to change. He unloaded his luggage and offboarded the plane.

Disembarking from the plane, Swapnil followed the signs to customs and immigration. The airport was bustling with activity, a mix of tourists, students, and locals. Swapnil now had to go through the immigration officer. He got in the line and saw many other migrants like him standing in the same queue looking tense. His turn came and he presented his documents, answering the immigration officer's questions with a blend of nervousness and anticipation. He cleared the customs with no hiccups, "phew, that felt intense," he chuckled to himself light-heartedly. After clearing customs, he stepped into the arrivals hall, feeling the cool breeze of Melbourne.

Swapnil's journey to Australia had been filled with excitement and anticipation. He had overcome the challenges of applying to universities, securing a visa, and saying emotional goodbyes to his loved ones. Each hurdle he cleared felt like a victory, bringing him one step closer to his dream. As he arrived in Melbourne, ready to begin his studies in data science at a prestigious university, Swapnil felt a sense of relief wash over him. He thought that the hardest part was behind him.

After all, he had already faced the daunting process of choosing the right course, navigating the maze of visa applications, and adjusting to the idea of leaving home for a new country. He had tackled these challenges head-on, believing that once he set foot in Australia, everything would fall into place. In his mind, the toughest battles had already been fought, and now it was time to enjoy the fruits of his labor.

He took a deep breath and made his way towards his accommodation for the day before heading to his university.

Chapter 5

The Start of a New Chapter

When Swapnil stepped out of the airport, he could feel a stark difference in his surroundings. His senses perceived a change in the atmosphere. The air felt different; it was crisper and cleaner. His hunch indicated that a huge shift was about to occur. Whether it was a premonition or an omen, he was yet to find out. He settled into his temporary accommodation comfortably and started planning the eventualities: He had to go to his university the next day morning. Swapnil was drained from the long journey, He decided on a long, sweet nap to relieve the exhaustion.

He woke up early the next morning, feeling refreshed after a good, long sleep. On his way to his university, he drifted into Melbourne's vibrant energy, and the promise of a world-class education filled Swapnil with confidence. He imagined his life would now be smooth sailing—focused on his studies, making new friends, and exploring all that Australia had to offer. The future seemed bright, and he was ready to embrace it without looking back.

Swapnil entered the gates of his university; he was mesmerized by the vast campus, the stunning architecture, and the sprawling greenery. He made his way into the university administration building to get his student ID card, a crucial step in officially starting his studies. The office was bustling with new students, each eager to begin their academic journey. Swapnil waited in line, his heart pounding with excitement.

When it was his turn, he approached the counter and handed over his documents to the receptionist. She examined his paperwork and then looked up with a concerned expression. "I'm sorry, but you only have a conditional offer. We need your final year results from your undergraduate degree. Without those, we can't issue your ID card, and if we don't receive them within the next seven days, your offer will be canceled."

Swapnil felt the ground slip from under his feet. The words echoed in his mind: "conditional offer," "canceled," "seven days." It was as if all his dreams were shattering before his eyes. He had come so far, and now everything was at risk because of a missing document.

In a daze, Swapnil left the administration office and returned to his room at his accommodation. Panic set in as he dialed his father's number. When his father answered, Swapnil's voice trembled with urgency. "Dad, please go to the college, go to the university, go anywhere, but get my result somehow. If my result doesn't come, my admission will be canceled. What will I say to my friends whom I gave a farewell to and posted selfies with on Facebook? My dreams have barely started and they are already shattered." He uttered in disbelief.

His father, sensing the desperation in his son's voice, assured him that he would do everything possible to get the results.

“Don't stress Swapnil, you've come this far, there’s no way you will have to give it all up to return home, it's just a small hiccup in the process. Have faith and stay calm beta,” his father asserted. The countdown began, and every passing day felt like an eternity.

Back in Delhi, Swapnil's father embarked on a relentless quest to obtain his son's final year results. He visited

Swapnil's college, spoke to administrators, and pleaded with officials. The process was slow and filled with bureaucratic hurdles, but he refused to give up. Meanwhile, Swapnil was in constant contact with his father, anxiously awaiting updates. Three to four days passed, each one filled with anxiety and sleepless nights. Swapnil tried to focus on settling into his new environment, but the uncertainty of his situation weighed heavily on him.

Finally, Swapnil's father managed to obtain the results and sent them over immediately. Swapnil received the email notification with a sense of relief and dread. He quickly downloaded the document, printed it out, and rushed back to the university administration office.

With only two days left before the deadline, Swapnil presented his final year results to the administration. The receptionist verified the document and finally issued him his student ID card. Swapnil breathed a sigh of relief; he had narrowly avoided disaster.

Feeling a mix of exhaustion and gratitude, Swapnil thanked the receptionist and made his way out of the building. He now had his official admission into the course, but his challenges were far from over.

Swapnil decided to apply for university accommodation, hoping to find a stable place to stay. He approached the accommodation desk and inquired about available options. The girl at the desk looked at him sympathetically and said, "Unfortunately, those applications closed three weeks ago. Those who already applied, please try next semester. There is no accommodation available at the university this semester."

Swapnil's heart sank. He had not anticipated this additional hurdle. With nowhere to stay, he felt lost and overwhelmed.

Desperate, he called his friend Jaiveer. "Bro, there is no place to stay," Swapnil said, his voice filled with despair.

Jaiveer, always supportive and resourceful, responded immediately, "Man, come stay with me for a few days. We will find something for you."

Swapnil felt a wave of relief wash over him. He packed his belongings and headed to Jaiveer's place. He caught a train, then a bus, and followed Google Maps to finally reach Jaiveer's house. Jaiveer was staying with his friends in an upmarket three-bedroom apartment with a sea view.

Swapnil was meeting Jaiveer in person after ages. As he approached a familiar-looking silhouette standing outside the apartment, on walking closer he began to see how different his close friend looked. It was almost as if he had a huge glow-up after moving to Melbourne for his undergrad. Swapnil thought Jaiveer carried himself with more suave and confidence, his styling and grooming was a sight to behold. Swapnil and Jaiveer walked toward each other gleaming in joy, both embraced each other tightly. It felt like they went back in time to when they were both just kids who had a lot of fun spending time together.

“It has been a long time Swapnil, I can't believe you're finally here,” stated Jaiveer.

“I promised I'd meet you soon, didn't I?” chuckled Swapnil.

Jaiveer guided Swapnil into his apartment; Swapnil was mesmerized by the posh locality the apartment was situated in and its proximity to the beach.

Swapnil looked around the apartment in awe; he was smitten by the lavish apartment. Jaiveer saw Swapnil’s reaction to his home and smiled. “Don't worry man, we'll get you a nice place like this one.” He said.

"Maybe not now, but sometime in the future that would be nice," Swapnil replied laughing.

Jaiveer welcomed Swapnil with open arms, he showed him around his house, and introduced him to his roommates. For the next two days, the two friends worked tirelessly to find Swapnil a permanent place to stay.

They scoured online listings, visited potential accommodations, and made countless phone calls. Despite the challenges, Swapnil was determined to find a suitable place. Jaiveer's support was invaluable during this time, offering not only a place to stay but also emotional encouragement.

After two days of relentless searching, Swapnil finally found a room in a shared apartment not too far from the university. The place was modest but clean, and the rent was within his budget. Swapnil moved in, feeling a mix of relief and excitement. He was grateful for Jaiveer's help and support during such a critical time. After securing his ID card and dealing with the accommodation crisis, Swapnil headed to Jaiveer's apartment. That night, they ordered food and drinks from a very expensive restaurant, costing 4,000-5,000 rupees. As they sat in the living room, enjoying the sumptuous meal, Jaiveer asked, "So, Swapnil, what's going on?"

Swapnil replied, "Man, I'm very stressed. I faced so many difficulties just for admission. How many more problems will come in the future?"

Jaiveer said, "It's amazing how many problems you faced. I didn't have to deal with any of that."

After talking for 15-20 minutes, Swapnil said, "I just need to complete this course somehow and secure a job because my dad mortgaged our only house to get a loan for my education."

Jaiveer replied, "Bro, my dad believes that education should be pursued with a free mind, so he paid all my fees and sent me here for graduation. Your situation is different. I came straight here and I'm doing a degree in liberal arts, where I don't have to stress at all."

Hearing Jaiveer's words, Swapnil was reminded of his childhood and the differences in their lives. He remembered how he used to come to school in an expensive car and how Jaiveer would always pay everyone's bill alone. When he had gone to Jaiveer's house for his birthday, he felt that 6000 people like him could fit into that house. Comparing himself to others, he realized that everyone's struggles are very different. This was the first time Swapnil felt that he might have rushed into coming abroad.

Swapnil now turned to Jaiveer looking to get more clarity about what his plans for the future were, now that he had finished his Bachelor's in Australia. Jaiveer had been in Melbourne for 4 years, and to Swapnil, he seemed like someone who had it all figured out—someone who had already mastered the city that was just beginning to unfold for him.

Jaiveer let out a deep breath, a small smile playing on his lips. "Yeah, Melbourne has been great. But after a while, the newness wears off."

Swapnil raised an eyebrow. "Really? You sound like you're already tired of it."

Jaiveer leaned back in his chair, running a hand through his perfectly styled hair. "I guess you could say that. I've been here for a few years now—did my undergrad, partied, and the usual. But it all feels too familiar now, like I've seen everything there is to see."

Swapnil tried to wrap his head around what Jaiveer was saying. "I find that hard to believe. You've been here so long; I thought you'd have it all figured out by now."

Jaiveer let out a light laugh. "That's the thing, though. I thought I'd have it figured out too. But I'm still not sure what I want to do with my life. So, I've decided to mix things up a bit. I'm thinking of doing my master's in Paris."

Swapnil nearly choked on his drink. "Paris? That's a big move, isn't it?"

Jaiveer shrugged, his eyes wandering to the city outside his apartment as if he could already see the streets of Paris laid out before him. "Maybe, but I need a change of scenery. Melbourne's great, but I'm bored. I've been here long enough to know it's time for something different."

Swapnil couldn't help but feel a pang of envy mixed with confusion. Here was Jaiveer, with all the freedom in the world, casually deciding to uproot his life on a whim. Meanwhile, Swapnil was just starting to find his footing in Melbourne. "But what about your career? Isn't moving to Paris a bit drastic just because you're bored?"

Jaiveer's smile broadened, but there was a hint of something deeper in his eyes—restlessness, maybe even uncertainty. "Probably, but that's just how I am. I'm always looking for the next big thing. Melbourne's been good, but it's not enough anymore. Maybe Paris will be different. Or maybe it won't. Either way, I'll figure it out."

The conversation left Swapnil feeling a little unsettled. He had come to Melbourne with a clear goal—to study, to build a career, to create a future. But listening to Jaiveer, he couldn't help but wonder if certainty was as fleeting as

Jaiveer made it seem. Was there a point where everything fell into place, or was life just a series of restless searches for something more?

Both of their eyes wandered off to the sea view, the waves crashing and pulling from the shore, the sound of the sea mixed with the wind's chime created a harmonious symphony which was an auditory pleasure. Both friends sat in sublime silence for a good couple of moments.

"I think Paris will be splendid for you Jai, you are the kind to settle in anywhere you go," said Swapnil, after processing the information he had just come to know from his dearest friend.

Jaiveer was taken aback; he hadn't expected Swapnil to tell him exactly what he wanted to hear. "Not sure about that, but it feels good to hear. Thanks, Swapnil." He replied warmly.

Swapnil smiled back at his friend. It was past sunset, and Swapnil took his leave after bidding his byes to Jaiveer and his roommates.

After parting with Swapnil, Jaiveer sat by himself, looking pensive. He contemplated on his life so far. He knew he was privileged from the get-go, but sometimes he felt like he did not have the opportunity to truly understand his passions and the extent of his potential. He had everything he always asked for, his needs were met and so were his desires. He did have ambitions, but nothing felt far out of reach, sometimes his privilege hindered him from finding his purpose in life. He was immensely grateful to have everything he wanted and beyond, but he felt empty at times. His social media only portrayed the side of his life he was keen on showing off to others, he hid his insecurities, doubts, and emptiness from the rest of the world. At times, he felt he had to keep up a facade to protect his true feelings.

Watching Swapnil strive to become someone and witnessing the yearning fire within him inspired Jai. He never mentioned it to him, but he looked up to his friend a lot. The recent conversation with Swapnil gave him a lot to ponder about, he decided that Paris would be the chapter of his life where he would take complete charge of his life and make something significant out of himself.

Chapter 6

The Unseen Struggles

Swapnil packed up his belongings to move into his shared apartment, with the help of Jaiveer he commuted to his new home and began unpacking. He tried to make it as homely as he could, he splurged on minimal room decor, a couple of house plants and set up his room.

After settling into his new accommodation, Swapnil's immediate concern shifted to securing a part-time job to cover his expenses. The money he had brought with him from India was rapidly depleting, and he knew that without a steady income, he wouldn't be able to sustain himself. He came to know of the part-time jobs within the college campus, he figured it would be a practical and ideal situation if he were to get a job within the campus. Swapnil started compiling a resume together and sent it out to apply for jobs.

Swapnil attended his classes diligently, taking rigorous notes and studying whenever he could find time. It was exciting for him to live out this opportunity surrounded by diverse students from all around the world who all brought forth a different perspective and nuance to the classes. However, He barely had the time to socialize and form close bonds with his batchmates. It took him quite a while to adjust to the curriculum and the lectures. The course was vast and the material that was prescribed or recommended was much more extensive. He was either spending his free time in the library or applying for part-time jobs when he wasn't occupied with chores such as grocery shopping, cooking, and cleaning. He had no time to socialize, let alone personal time to himself.

He wanted to stay on top of his academics and try to make the best out of this opportunity. “I'm past all the hurdles now, I'll just have to get a part-time job now, and I'll be pretty set,” he thought to himself. As each day passed away he was flooded with rejections from part-time job placements at his campus.

Initially, Swapnil was optimistic. He believed he would easily find a good part-time job at the university. However, reality soon struck as rejection after rejection poured in. He realized it would be quite difficult to get a job within the campus. He decided to broaden his scope and started to apply for jobs anywhere he found vacancies. After his classes, all he did was scour through sources and references to find a job opening.

He had applied for every available position, from working in the university cafeteria to being a library assistant, but none materialized. He expanded his search beyond the university, applying to grocery stores, cafes, and even car washes. Each rejection chipped away at his confidence, leaving him increasingly despondent.

Day in and day out, it felt like a tiresome rut. He dreaded checking emails and callbacks from job applications as they usually carried the news of his job rejection. It was starting to get overwhelming with his dwindling finances.

One afternoon, after his classes, he found a quiet place on the campus lawn under a tree. He sat down, leaning against a tree. He got a call from his father.

“How are you beta? Is everything good?” His father asked.

“Yes papa, everything is fine, how are you and Ma?” Swapnil replied

"We're good Swapnil, we just wanted to check up on you. Remember we're always here for you no matter what, if you need anything don't hesitate to call us." His father stated, trying not to well up with emotions.

Swapnil did not want to tell his parents about his financial situation. He grinned and responded, "There's absolutely nothing to worry about papa, I've applied to a couple of part-time jobs, and I'm pretty confident about getting a job. Academics is going well too." He wanted to confide in his parents desperately, but he felt it would affect them more than it did him.

"We are more than happy to send you some money so you can settle in comfortably, at least till you find a good part time job," Swapnil's father proclaimed.

"It's fine papa, I'm able to manage everything well, don't stress," he replied, concealing his fraught circumstances. Swapnil was not comfortable depending on his family for money, he knew how much of a financial strain they were under, since his move abroad.

They said their byes and hung up the call, leaving Swapnil dwelling on his circumstances. Ever since he had stepped foot in Melbourne, he felt as though he was treading through one hurdle after another. He kept hoping it would get better each day but, every day felt like a test of his persistence. The fact that Swapnil was swamped with his grueling schedule and missed out on socializing did not help the fact that he was starting to feel overcome with isolation and melancholy. The cultural shock was also another huge aspect.

It dawned upon him that his expectations might not exactly play out the way that he had imagined once he moved to a foreign country. He had all the freedom that he ever wanted, but he also felt the crushing pressure of overbearing responsibilities.

One day, as he was heading home after classes, his phone rang. It was an unknown number. With a mixture of hope and dread, Swapnil answered. The voice on the other end informed him that he had been selected for a job at a local car wash. Swapnil was floored, he was not expecting an offer, especially with the long line of rejections he was thrust into.

"Thank you so much for the opportunity! Could I have more details regarding the job description and the pay, please? He asked.

The person on the other side of the call gave him a detailed structure of the job description, hours, and pay. The relief was palpable, however, it came with a caveat: the job was cash-in-hand, meaning it was off the books and wouldn't provide any job security or benefits. But none of it mattered to Swapnil, with barely a negligible amount left in his bank account he was desperate for any job he could get his hands on.

Despite the job profile and the low security it offered, Swapnil accepted the job. It wasn't what he had dreamed of, but at least he had a way to earn money. The job required hard work and long hours, but he was grateful for the opportunity to support himself.

He excitedly called up Jaiveer to inform him about the new job,

"Jai, I just got a call from a local car wash, they're willing to keep me for the part-time job! I know it is not what I had envisioned but something is better than nothing isn't it?" He said giddily.

Jaiveer was astounded by Swapnil's drive, "That's great man, you have the hustle in you! I'm glad you're doing this, with time it will get better Swapnil, always keep at it. I'm proud of you," he stated.

Swapnil was finally relieved, he no longer had the mounting stress of finances upon him. He conversed with Jaiveer for a while and later called up his family to share the news about his part-time employment. However, he told them that he had been offered a part-time admin job, instead of disclosing that it was a job at the local car wash. He didn't want his parents to learn of the struggles he was going through, he felt if he were honest with him about his actual job description they would be on edge with worry. His family was skeptical, they told him not to burden himself with additional worries and responsibilities and asked him to focus on his academics. He told his parents not to worry too much and that he would always keep his academics at the top of his priorities. After a warm conversation with his parents, he got back to finishing up his coursework.

Fifteen days before his exams, Swapnil started his job at the car wash. When he went in and met the owner of the car wash, he was introduced to the rest of the workers and briefed about the job. He had flexible work hours as the pay depended on the work hours he put in. However, it did seem quite physically taxing. He changed into his workwear and started the job.

After the first day at work, Swapnil was worn out. He was not accustomed to physically demanding activity for long hours. His body felt sore and he wanted to rest up, but he reminded himself he had an exam coming up soon and he mustered up the strength to sit through a thorough study session. After pushing himself that night Swapnil dozed off the moment his body hit the bed.

His schedule became punishing. He worked from 5 to 9 in the morning, attended university classes from 9 to 4, prepared for his upcoming exams, wrapped up his assignments from 4 to 6, and then worked again until 9 at night. By the time he returned home, he was taken over by sheer exhaustion.

Each morning felt like an intense drill, the blaring alarm every morning felt like torture with the weather outside. He loved to sleep in for a long time back when he was in his undergrad. The only times he woke up early was around exams, he thought to himself of how easy he had it back in Delhi. He didn't have to worry about his meals, commute, or finances. Just in over a couple of months, his life had taken a drastic turn. He was obligated to cook his own meals as eating out often was a very expensive option, he had to find time for grocery shopping, looking up recipes and prepping for meals. More than often, his eating schedule and frequency of meals he consumed were compromised. Washing the dishes, doing the laundry, cleaning his space, and organizing also took up a significant chunk of Swapnils time. Back home he was accustomed to his mother cooking fresh meals for him, at his university he managed with mess food and other instant foods he had stocked up on. Cleaning was another huge challenge that he had to navigate, he had to get accustomed to cleaning up after himself regularly, if he skipped a day's worth of cleaning he was faced with a piling rack of unwashed dishes, a mound of laundry or clutter all over his space.

The physical demands of the job were significant. Washing cars involved constant bending, scrubbing, and lifting, which took a toll on his body. The early mornings were particularly tough, especially as winter approached and the mornings grew colder. Swapnil often found himself shivering as he worked, but he pushed through, driven by the need to survive.

He had to constantly remind himself that things would eventually get better, but as the days grew colder it grew tougher to have unwavering hope. He was worn out by the end of the day trying to balance work, academics, and household.

As the days passed, he began conversing with people around him more openly. He felt more comfortable as time went by and began forming bonds with people from his classes and the car wash job. The routine was tiring, but rewarding. His confidence hit a positive curve, especially when he received his first paycheck. It felt tremendously gratifying to know that he was able to sustain himself financially in a completely foreign country with not many familiar faces around him. Each day he discovered something new about himself and his limits, he saw himself catapult into a hardworking and resilient person each time he was put through an arduous situation.

Days grew harder but his resolution grew stronger, he pushed himself at every facet of his newfound life and began exploring himself inwardly. He decided to take each day by stride and remain consistent and committed to his choice of coming to Melbourne for his education.

Chapter 7

Alone in the Storm

Swapnil hazily opened his eyes, surprised the alarm hadn't awakened him yet. Yesterday's car wash hours had taken a toll on his body and he was feeling sore and groggy, he frantically looked around for his phone, with his hands wandering around the bed trying to grasp a hold of his device. He unlocked his phone and, with half eyes closed, looked at the time, and jumped off his bed. He was late for his class. He quickly dressed up and rushed out of his apartment berserkly.

Swapnil headed to his class, pacing hastily toward his lecture hall, hoping to get to his class as soon as he possibly could. Exasperated with his delay, he tried to sprint across with his bag. Unfortunately for Swapnil, he missed a pothole that sent him flying across. The thud sent throbbing pain across the parts of his body that took the hit, pumped with adrenaline, he skittishly looked around to comprehend what had just happened to him. He felt unbearable pain trying to lift his body from the fall. As he tried to get up through pain he slowly reached for his bag and books that lay all across the street. As he slowly tried to move, he felt a sharp pain in his left ankle. Even after trying hard, he could not put any weight on it. He realized through pain that he had twisted his ankle and there was no way he could make it to class. He slowly hobbled back to his apartment, pushing through the pain.

As Swapnil hobbled into his small apartment, each step sent a sharp pang through his twisted ankle. The once routine walk back from campus had turned into an excruciating ordeal after he had tripped on an uneven pavement. He managed to unlock the door in a panicked state of mind, he sighed a wave of relief as he collapsed onto the couch, wincing as he carefully removed his shoe. The swelling was already noticeable, and he knew he needed medical attention, but the thought of going through the process alone made him feel more isolated than ever.

He glanced around his sparsely furnished apartment, where the only sound was the quiet hum of the refrigerator and the distant murmur of the city outside. Melbourne had been full of promise when he arrived—new adventures, a fresh start, and endless opportunities. But tonight, it felt like a cold, indifferent place. The loneliness of being a foreign student, juggling studies and part-time work, had never felt as heavy as it did now.

Swapnil sighed, reaching for his phone. He dialed the number of a local clinic he had found online. After a brief wait, he was given an appointment for later that evening. He struggled to his feet, leaning heavily on a makeshift crutch made from a broom handle, and slowly made his way out the door.

The journey to the clinic felt intense, Swapnil's mind was turbulent with strong feelings. Being physically hurt and alone in a new city was not in his cards when he had envisioned a life in Melbourne. The clinic's sterile smell and the impersonal buzz of fluorescent lights only deepened his sense of isolation. He filled out forms with one hand, the other clinging to his crutch for support. The receptionist, polite but detached, directed him to a waiting area. As he sat down, Swapnil glanced at the other patients—some chatting with companions, others lost in their own thoughts. He was the only one here alone.

When his name was finally called, he limped into the examination room. The doctor, though kind, carried out the examination with clinical efficiency. Swapnil winced through the procedure as the doctor confirmed the ankle was sprained, and he would need to wear a brace and undergo physical therapy. The entire time, he felt the cold sting of solitude. His ankle looked really bad, it had turned into all shades of pink, purple, and blue. He gazed at his foot in turmoil as the nurse installed a brace on it. He hobbled along and got out of the room.

The nurse glanced at him and asked him, “Have you brought anyone along with you? Looks like you might need assistance getting back home.”

“Umm, I'm here by myself, but I'll be able to manage, thanks for asking,” sighed Swapnil. The nurse's comment felt like salt rubbing into his wounds.

The nurse smiled at him pitifully, feeling for Swapnil. She helped him walk up to the clinic door.

As he left the clinic with a cumbersome brace on his ankle, Swapnil felt a wave of helplessness. The city, which had seemed so full of possibilities, now felt like a vast expanse with no one to turn to. His part-time job would be difficult with the injury, and managing his studies with a brace would be another challenge. His thoughts began spiraling in his head, he felt burdened and vulnerable, and he felt like he had no shoulder to lean on.

Back in his apartment, Swapnil sat on the couch, feeling the weight of his loneliness pressing down on him. He wanted to call his parents, to hear a comforting voice and share his struggles. But he knew they would worry too much. They had already sacrificed so much for his education abroad. The last thing he wanted was to add to their burdens with his problems.

Instead, he sent a brief text to a few friends, downplaying the severity of his situation. He didn't want to worry them either, and he knew they had their own set of troubles that preoccupied them. As he lay back, staring at the ceiling, the silence of his apartment was a stark reminder of how alone he felt.

The nights in Melbourne had been filled with dreams of success and new beginnings, but tonight, as he struggled with his injury and isolation, those dreams seemed distant and unreachable. He was learning the hard way that even amidst the promise of a new life, there could be moments of profound loneliness. The idle days of rest fed into Swapnil's intrusive thoughts. He now not only had to deal with physically taxing activities but also his depleting mental health.

Yet, deep down, Swapnil knew he had to push through. This was just one more challenge in a journey that was far from over.

With a heavy heart and an aching ankle, he closed his eyes, hoping that tomorrow would bring a glimmer of hope and perhaps a bit of solace in the vast expanse of his new world.

A few days later, while he was recovering from his injury, Swapnil realized that he had no time to waste and got back to his daily routine. It took much of a mental effort than a physical one for him to get back to his usual routine, the days of recovery weighed heavy on his mental well-being, and Swapnil was on the verge of a huge breakdown.

Despite his grueling schedule, Swapnil remained determined to succeed in his studies. He attended every lecture, completed his assignments, and prepared diligently for his exams. Balancing work and academics was incredibly challenging. He often found himself dozing off in class, his eyelids heavy from lack of sleep. He pushed ahead, constantly reminding himself of the choices he had made out of his own will, persistence was a character of his that didn't easily go away, even after coming to Melbourne.

As the days passed, His professors noticed his fatigue but didn't know the full extent of his struggles. They noticed his strained demeanor, and struggle to keep up with the ongoing lectures. On many occasions they tried to converse with Swapnil, hoping to understand what was happening to him. Nonetheless, Swapnil did not want to share his hardships, preferring to keep his problems to himself. He feared that revealing his struggles might be seen as a sign of weakness.

One of the hardest aspects of Swapnil's new life was the isolation. His job left him with no time or money to socialize. His friend Jaiveer, who had been a constant source of support, continued to call him daily, inviting him to parties and outings.

"Hey man, how are you doing? Are you off the crutch now? Jaiveer asked, on the phone call with Swapnil.

"I'm good jai, I've recovered fine now," replied Swapnil.

"That's great man, listen, there's a party happening next week at a friend's house, it's going to be huge! I think you should come, I want you to come. You can't decline this time Swapnil," chuckled Jaiveer.

"I would love to, but I'm just very busy right now Jai, I appreciate the invite though," he answered, sighing. He wanted to go out, but his circumstances were cramped. He felt bad about declining Jaiveer's invite for the umpteenth time.

"That's cool man, let me know when you would be down to hang out," said an upset Jai. Jaiveer did not know the whole extent of Swapnil's problems, he felt bad about Swapnil frequently bailing out of plans, especially with him leaving for Paris soon.

"There's a party here, let's go," or "I'm going to this place, let's go," Jaiveer would say. In attempts to help his friend get out of his rut and let loose.

Swapnil always had to decline. "Sorry, Jaiveer, I can't. I have work," he would reply. Over time, the invitations became fewer, and Swapnil's social life dwindled to almost nothing. The thought of having friends or a social life didn't even cross his mind. His focus was solely on surviving and succeeding in his studies.

Late one night, after a particularly exhausting day, Swapnil sat on his bed, reflecting on his journey. He thought about the sacrifices his family had made to send him abroad. His father had mortgaged their house to secure a loan for his education, and Swapnil felt the weight of their expectations on his shoulders. He couldn't afford to fail. The pressure was immense, but it also fueled his determination.

He thought about Jaiveer's easygoing lifestyle and the stark contrast to his own. Jaiveer's father had paid for his education, allowing him to pursue his studies without financial worries. Swapnil realized that everyone's struggles were different. He had chosen a harder path, but he believed that his experiences would make him stronger and more resilient.

As the days turned into weeks, Swapnil's routine became a relentless cycle of work and study. Each day started before dawn, with the shrill sound of his alarm clock piercing the silence. He would groggily get out of bed, dress warmly, and head to the car wash. The mornings were particularly tough, with the cold air biting at his skin as he worked.

At the car wash, he scrubbed and rinsed cars, his muscles aching from the repetitive motions. The work was physically demanding, but Swapnil took pride in doing his job well. He knew that his earnings, though meager, were essential for his survival.

After his morning shift, he would rush to the university, often grabbing a quick bite to eat on the way. His classes required his full attention, and despite his fatigue, Swapnil remained focused. He took diligent notes, participated in discussions, and sought help from his professors when needed.

As his exams approached, Swapnil's anxiety grew. He knew that his academic performance was crucial for his future. After classes, he would head to the library, where he spent hours studying. His textbooks and notes became his constant companions, and he immersed himself in his studies. His only priority and focus shifted toward his academic performance. Swapnil felt like he had to put in his all to be able to score well, especially with a foreign and vast curriculum.

The stress of balancing work and academics was overwhelming. There were moments when Swapnil felt like giving up, but he reminded himself of his goals and the sacrifices his family had made. He couldn't afford to fail. Day in and out, he consistently stuck to his study schedule, took up fewer hours of work at the car wash, and studied whenever he found any spare time.

It was arduous, intense, and difficult, Swapnil had a firm belief in his hard work, growing up he was conditioned to believe that hard work always beats talent. This notion fueled his commitment; he wanted to make the best out of his situation instead of delving into all the circumstances that had gone awry and not in his favor. He persisted every day, till the days of his exams, giving his studies his ultimate dedication and focus.

Chapter 8

Unseen Bonds and Hidden Struggles

Swapnil's life in Melbourne was a constant hustle, balancing his demanding schedule of work and studies. His job at the car wash, though physically taxing, provided him with a steady income to cover his basic expenses. It was here, amidst the suds and grime of car washing, that Swapnil made a friend named Armaan.

Armaan was a cheerful and friendly presence at the car wash. Despite the harsh conditions and low pay, he always had a smile on his face. Swapnil appreciated Armaan's positive attitude, which made the long hours more bearable. They often chatted during breaks, sharing stories and jokes to lighten the workload.

On an unassuming afternoon, Swapnil came in to work early; he wanted to get in more hours of work as his exams had concluded. He greeted his friend, Armaan. Armaan waved back at Swapnil with a wide grin on his face.

"You're early today, good for me," Armaan chirped.

"Just trying to get my hours in," chuckled Swapnil.

"How did your exams go? You really had a tough time there didn't you, especially with the fall and everything," Armaan asked concernedly.

"It was definitely hard, but nothing I can't salvage," winked Swapnil with glimmer in his eyes.

It was definitely an arduous period for him, he was grateful to be done with it. He liked dealing with difficult experiences through humor, especially with his friends.

Both were inseparable during the work hours, their camaraderie while working and their fun and frolic during their breaks felt like a much needed break from reality for Swapnil. The banter and fun kept him distracted from the physical exhaustion from all the labor.

They both usually took their breaks together. On a certain break, both of them got together habitually, sharing how their day went and talking about their interests. As swapnil scrolled down his social media while showing a post to Armaan, Armaan's eyes lit up when he saw Jaiveer's post on the feed. "Wait, stop scrolling!" He exclaimed.

Swapnil was confused and retorted back, "do you know him?"

Armaan had a twinkle in his eyes as he responded, "of course I do! How do you know Veer?" Pointing at the screen.

Swapnil smiled. "Veer was my school friend. We've known each other for years."

Armaan's excitement grew. "I follow Jaiveer on social media. When I first saw him, I dreamt of studying abroad too."

Jaiveer had a tremendous following on his social media, owing to his well kempt and aesthetic posts portraying his lavish life in Melbourne. It was not that surprising to Swapnil that Armaan knew Jaiveer. A lot of Indian diaspora and Indian students aspiring to study or move abroad followed Jai. He portrayed the ideal lifestyle that served as an inspiration for all those who wanted the same for themselves.

Until that moment, Swapnil had never really asked Armaan about his background. He knew of Armaan his free spirited and fun loving nature, and all his interests besides academics and work, Armaan loved to talk, he aways had a lot to share, however, Swapnil did not recount anytime where Armaan mentioned his past and present state of affairs. His curiosity piqued, Swapnil asked, "How did you come here to study? What's your story?"

Armaan stopped smiling, a solemn demeanor took over him. Both Swapnil and him walked side by side as he began narrating his story.

Armaan began telling Swapnil everything from the beginning, from his childhood to his present day situation. He belonged to the Jalandhar area in Punjab. Since childhood, he had seen many people around him go to Canada, Australia, and the UK. Their lives seemed to transform after they moved abroad. They posted beautiful photos, received good marriage proposals, earned in foreign currencies, sent money home, and even built water tanks on their roofs with the money they made.

Armaan was pursuing a BCom degree from Punjab University when he first came across Jaiveer's social media account. Jaiveer lived in Australia, leading the life Armaan had always dreamed of. With 10,000 followers on Instagram, Jayveer's posts were filled with images of a life that seemed idyllic and prosperous. Armaan was one of those followers, captivated by the promise of a better life abroad.

Armaan's father, a farmer, had different aspirations for his son. He wanted Armaan to complete his BCom, get a private job, marry well, and settle down. The family had just enough money to get by, no more, no less. However, seeing kids go abroad and the allure of Jayveer's Instagram posts sparked a curiosity in Armaan. He was determined to go to Australia, no matter the cost.

Armaan managed to secure a student visa and moved to Melbourne, full of hope and dreams. But the reality was far from what he had imagined. He struggled with his studies and found it difficult to manage financially. Two years ago, his visa expired, and he had been living illegally in Australia ever since. He probably never completed his diploma. Due to his illegal status, he was paid half of what he should be earning at the car wash. He sent most of his earnings back home, supporting his family and maintaining the facade of a successful life abroad.

Swapnil listened in shock as Armaan recounted his struggles. The facade that Armaan presented to his family back home was a stark contrast to his harsh reality. Armaan said, "Whenever my family calls, I always tell them that life is going great here."

Swapnil couldn't help but admire Armaan's resilience but was also deeply concerned. "Why don't you just go back home? If you get a job, maybe you can save your farmland too," he suggested.

Armaan shook his head vehemently. "No, now this is it. Going back is not an option anymore. What face will I show when I go back home? I'll just earn some money here and send it home. Life will go on. You will get ahead because having a proper visa is such a big deal."

Swapnil felt a pang of empathy for Armaan. He realized how fortunate he was to have a proper visa. "Yeah, if you get permanent residency, everything will be sorted here," Armaan said, echoing Swapnil's thoughts.

Swapnil respected the aspect that Armaan kept his facade going only for the sake of his family, he could relate with him in this attribute. He too, like Armaan, cared immensely for his family. This got him thinking of his own family and how he probably would have done the same thing if he was in Armaan's situation, contrary to his advice to Armaan.

Armaan then shared his plan to try and get a visa by becoming a refugee through some dubious means. This revelation struck Swapnil deeply, reminding him of his own precarious situation. After his student visa, he only had a two-year visa. He too needed to start thinking about his future and the possibility of securing permanent residency.

The conversation with Armaan put a different perspective onto Swapnil's outlook, he couldn't imagine a man of Armaan's conduct, always jovial and lighthearted to have such a grim past. It felt absurd, Swapnil himself had recently gone through a significant ordeal after his arrival in Melbourne. He thought he had it really bad until this conversation with Armaan, Swapnil looked at his friend with deep empathy in his eyes.

"No matter what happens, I'll stick by your side," he proclaimed.

Armaans face mellowed with gratitude, "thank you Swapnil, you're a really nice person," he replied.

It had been a while since he had felt home with anyone, Armaan knew it would be quite a long time since he could see his family again, Swapnil, with his familiar ethnic background felt like a brother to him.

Swapnil, on the contrary, recognized the need of companionship and camaraderie amongst those going through similar, albeit, varied circumstances. Nobody from this foreign country could understand the struggles they had to face, it was hard and taxing, but they had no other choice but to push through, until they saw light at the end of the tunnel. The real question, however, stood strong, is there even a end to this arduous tunnel they were voyaging through?

The shrill winter grew deeper, days turned into weeks, and the car wash job continued to be a relentless grind for both Swapnil and Armaan. Despite the physical exhaustion, Swapnil found solace in their growing friendship. They supported each other through the tough times, sharing laughs and stories during their breaks. Armaan's cheerful disposition was infectious, and his resilience in the face of adversity inspired Swapnil.

Swapnil wished he could do something to help his friends situation, but he was also aware of how serious his situation was. it was a precarious scenario which would lead to bleak consequences, all Swapnil could do was to be there for Armaan as his confidante and support system.

Both learnt valuable lessons in strength and resilience in each other. Swapnil admired Armaan's tenacity, while, Armaan recognized the budding brilliance and strength in Swapnil.

Swapnil's schedule remained grueling. He continued to work from 5 to 9 in the morning, attended university classes from 9 to 4, studied from 4 to 6, and then worked again until 11 at night. The physical and mental toll was immense, but Swapnil was determined to succeed.

His conversation with Armaan also served as a persistent reminder of how hard he would have to strive to be able to secure a visa. It jolted Swapnil back into action whenever he slacked, the reality that would unfold if he was unable to secure the visa was daunting to even imagine.

His professors noticed his fatigue but admired his dedication. Swapnil sought help when needed, and his professors provided guidance and support. He relentlessly relied on his classmates and professors whenever he was not able to cope with the lectures. He realized asking for help wasn't a sign of weakness, it was a sign that he was comfortable relying on others and trusting in the power of community. He noticed that improved learning in a college setting could only happen through interactive feedback and reforms, involving others perspectives which in turn built holistic learning.

Despite the challenges, Swapnil's grades improved, and he felt more confident about his future.

Late one night, after a particularly exhausting day, Swapnil sat on his bed, reflecting on his journey. He thought about the sacrifices his family had made to send him abroad. His father had mortgaged their house to secure a loan for his education, and Swapnil felt the weight of their expectations on his shoulders. He couldn't afford to fail. The pressure was immense, but it also fueled his determination.

He thought about Jaiveer's easygoing lifestyle and the stark contrast to his own. Jaiveer's father had paid for his education, allowing him to pursue his studies without financial worries. Swapnil realized that everyone's struggles were different. He had chosen a harder path, but he believed that his experiences would make him stronger and more resilient.

The two contrasting experiences of his dear friends, Jaiveer and Armaan, helped Swapnil understand the spectrum of outcomes of his situation. Both had the same dreams and aspirations, however, the way their lives unfurled were drastically different. On one hand, Jaiveer was probably busy throwing another party at his house at the moment, inviting all his acquaintances and building his network. On the flipside, Armaan might have been busy scrubbing stubborn stains off a car, asking the car wash owner if he could take up more hours to be able to send his family more money for upcoming festivals. The stark dissimilarities in their turn of events helped Swapnil build a thorough perspective, helping him remain in a state of gratitude. His life was his own to navigate; he realized that the circumstances and the environment he had been in so far did not have to dictate the rest of his life. He wanted to be the owner of his trajectory and build something so infallible that external circumstances would not be able to falter him.

His ambitions remained steadfast, the past hindrances did not bother him anymore, infect, and they served him as a reminder of his strength and persistence.

Chapter 9

Ambition and Action

Time flew by fast, Swapnil was engrossed with his academics and his part-time job. Before he could completely submerge himself into Melbourne's culture and lifestyle, he was already in his final year of the master's program. Seasons changed, and so did the people in his life. It was difficult to find solace in stagnation when fleeting moments and change were the only ones he could find respite in. Swapnil's academics saw a dip in his performance, he found himself falling behind in his final year. He was confused and in despair "My grades aren't getting any better, I need to start putting in more effort," he thought to himself. But, at the back of his mind, he was aware of how hard it would be to dedicate a significant chunk of his time to his academics, given his work and chores.

At lectures, his professors noticed Swapnil's declining academic performance. A kind professor decided to intervene; he partially knew the struggles of foreign students and was keen on helping Swapnil.

After the class, Swapnil approached his professor to clear a couple of doubts, his professor gladly helped him out and asked him if everything was fine. Swapnil replied nonchalantly, answering that he had just been feeling under the weather for the past few weeks, he was not eager to share his problems with his professor, he adamantly liked keeping things to himself unless it was an absolute necessity to share the happenings in his life. The professor sensed the hesitation in Swapnil's answer. "I think you should approach Vedant, he might be able to understand some of the things you're going through and help you out academically." Vedant was the class topper known for his meticulous notes and academic excellence, Swapnil knew him briefly because of his academic prowess and mutuals in their friend group, however, he had not interacted with Vedant beyond casual greetings and small talk.

After class one day, Swapnil mustered the courage to approach Vedant and ask for his assistance. He walked up to Vedant and waved at him.

"Hey Vedant, do you mind sharing your notes with me? I'm struggling to keep up," Swapnil said, hoping his request didn't come across as too desperate.

Vedant greeted Swapnil back, smiling warmly. "Of course, Swapnil. I'd be happy to help. But may I ask why you're having trouble? Is everything okay?" He asked.

Swapnil hesitated, unsure if he should share his struggles with Vedant. But then he decided to open up. "I've been working at a car wash to cover my expenses, and it's been taking a toll on my studies." Swapnil answered. It was unusual for him to share about his struggles with someone he was barely acquainted with, but Vedant had a welcoming and friendly energy that got Swapnil comfortable.

Vedant nodded sympathetically. "I understand, but I believe you should focus more on your studies as of now. Have you considered looking for volunteering opportunities instead? It could open up more doors for you."

Swapnil was surprised by Vedant's suggestion, from what he inferred it seemed like Vedant did not have a part time job to support himself. "But how do you manage without a part-time job?" He asked, curious about Vedant's seemingly sorted situation.

Vedant chuckled. “I don’t need a part-time job. I’m here on a 100% scholarship.”

Swapnil’s eyes widened in surprise. He was in awe and wanted to get to know Vedant better. Swapnil thanked Vedant and parted ways. He felt Vedant was an interesting person.

The next day, he ran into Vedant again, on his way to the campus cafeteria. He waved at him from a distance and approached him. “Hi man, where are you headed?” He asked Vedant.

Vedant waved and answered, “I'm headed to the cafeteria, are you headed the same way?”

“Yes, just got done with revising some notes, I'll join you,” Swapnil replied.

As they both headed together, Swapnil’s curiosity got the best of him.

“A scholarship? How did you manage that?” He asked Vedant, still in awe and surprise.

Vedant replied, laughing “It's a long story, and it was quite unexpected.”

“Go ahead, I have quite a lot of time to spare at the moment,” Swapnil chuckled.

“Tell me everything from scratch, where are you from? What's your story?” He nudged Vedant. Swapnil saw him as a very peculiar yet mysterious person. Vedant wasn't known for being talkative, there was often an air of suspense around him.

Both of them grabbed a couple of refreshments and sat on a table. Vedant began narrating his story from the beginning

He belonged to the Nagpur area of Maharashtra and had excelled in academics from a young age. Despite financial constraints after his father's passing, Vedant's mother worked tirelessly to support him and his two sisters through school. College education seemed like a distant dream, but Vedant remained determined to succeed.

Swapnil empathized with Vedant. He couldn't imagine how hard it must have been for Vedant growing up without a father. He thought of his own father and reflected on how his father had played a tremendous role in his education in Melbourne.

"My luck hit a jackpot only during college though! It felt grim until I was studying computer science engineering at Mumbai University. I was scoring quite well in all exams and tests, I also won a couple of accolades here and there which helped I guess." He claimed, sheepishly.

Though it was obvious to Swapnil that Vedant was attempting to be humble about his accomplishments, there was no doubt that he was an upstanding student in his undergrad.

"When was the moment you hit the jackpot?" Swapnil smirked, teasing Vedant.

"So during an exchange program, a couple of representatives from the Australian university noticed some of the projects I was working on. They were quite intrigued so we had a bit of tete-a-tete. After the meeting ended, one of them approached me and told me that they would like to extend an admission offer with a hundred percent scholarship. That's when things took a major turn for me. I am very grateful for the opportunities I have had along the way," he replied with gratitude in his tone.

Swapnil was amazed at how Vedant's destiny had unfurled, "that's great man! I'm proud of you. Don't give all the credit to the opportunities though, it seems like you really did make the best out of all the opportunities that came your way," said Swapnil, encouragingly.

Vedant tried to brush it off shyly, "it's nothing, we both have much more to accomplish," he stated.

Swapnil nodded in agreement, his conversations with Vedant always gave him abundant hope and inspiration.

Even before finishing his final year, Vedant had received a lucrative job offer from the university, along with assurances of permanent residency sponsorship. His hard work and dedication had paid off, securing him a bright future.

Vedant's humble beginnings to his journey to a seamless abroad education felt surreal, Swapnil was awestruck and continued to listen to him eagerly.

"That's how I'm here, if it wasn't for all the things that happened when I was growing up, I probably wouldn't be here sitting next to you. I owe a lot of credit to my mother and education," he added.

Swapnil listened to Vedant's story with a mix of inspiration and envy. "Your situation is so sorted. I don't even know what I'll do," he admitted.

Vedant looked at Swapnil and thought for a while, "I'm going to tell you something that might come off too strong, but I really think you should think about it," he insisted while taking a sip from his coffee.

"Sure man, tell me, I'm all ears." Swapnil replied, inquisitively. Longing to hear what Vedant felt about his circumstances and plight.

Vedant offered some sage advice. "As of now, I feel like you should focus entirely on your final year exams. Look for good volunteering opportunities in your spare time, this will drastically open up new avenues for you. Build your portfolio, and secure a job that pays well. This will open the path to permanent residency."

Swapnil mulled over Vedant's advice, it did seem like a foolproof suggestion. His only concern was how he would manage his temporary needs if he were to shift his focus on building his future. He and Vedant talked for a long time, they shared their thoughts on varied topics and reminisced about their lives back in India, their similar ethnicities were an added perk to their budding friendship.

From that day on, Swapnil made a commitment to prioritize his studies. He started searching for volunteering opportunities to gain practical experience and enhance his resume.

He realized if he exerted all of his energy on getting by day to day, he would miss out on the bigger picture. The ultimate goal was that of permanent residency, Armaas's story echoed in his head. He saw his friend's predicament, and he did not want that for himself. He reflected on his journey so far and wanted all of his hard work to culminate into something fruitful.

In his quest for volunteering opportunities, Swapnil came across an organization that caught his eye. He joined a social justice group at his college. The group was dedicated to advocating for marginalized communities and fighting for social change. He resonated with the cause and was devoted to giving this opportunity his best efforts. Swapnil threw himself into various activities, organizing campaigns, rallies, and distributing food to the poor every Saturday and Sunday.

It was a humongous bit of work, but it did not feel as lonely as the car wash job, as he had other passionate individuals accompanying him in the venture. It was after a long time he was finally getting along with his college mates, earlier he barely was part of suitable occasions to converse and socialize with them. He was thoroughly submerged in his part-time job and academics. This opportunity felt like a fresh breath of air in comparison to all the recent ordeals he had been through.

Initially, Swapnil didn't fully understand the significance of these activities. But he remembered Vedant's advice – every experience could potentially lead to bigger opportunities in the future. He saw this as a chance to socialize and also build a sense of purpose within him.

As Swapnil became more involved in the group's activities, he discovered a strong sense of purpose and fulfillment that he hadn't felt before. Working alongside like-minded individuals who were passionate about social justice opened his eyes to the issues facing society and inspired him to make a difference. He went into the volunteering opportunity looking it as an addition to his resume, but each day working towards the cause gave him much more than he had initially envisioned and anticipated.

He found himself becoming more confident and outspoken, advocating for causes he believed in and challenging injustice wherever he saw it. The sense of camaraderie within the group was empowering, and Swapnil felt a sense of belonging that he had never experienced before.

Through his involvement in the social justice group, Swapnil gained valuable skills and experience that would prove invaluable in his future career. He learned how to organize events, communicate effectively, and work collaboratively with others toward a common goal.

Swapnil also honed his leadership abilities, taking on roles of responsibility within the group and learning how to motivate and inspire others. These experiences helped him grow both personally and professionally, preparing him for the challenges that lay ahead.

The experience was enriching and invaluable, just like Vedant had previously told him. After his classes, Vedant and Swapnil often hung out for a while, both saw the immense potential in one another and motivated each other to become the best versions of themselves. They talked about everything under the sun, ranging from their academic progress, and current affairs in the world to their personal lives.

One day, Swapnil and Vedant sat on the lawn, basking under the shallow rays of sun permeating through the crevices of the tree's foliage.

Swapnil was lying down and Vedant was sitting, leaning onto the trunk of a tree beside him. Vedant looked at Swapnil and remarked "I'm starting to see significant changes in you ever since you joined the volunteering group"

"What do you mean? How have I changed?" A perplexed Swapnil asked.

Vedant giggled, "Don't worry, it's a good change, you seem more confident and efficient, I can see the drive in you. It finally looks like you're serious about your career now," he said.

"Maybe I have, or maybe I always was and just needed an outlet to feel like myself again." Swapnil chimed in.

Both of them smiled at each other and began discussing the lecture they had together earlier that day.

As Swapnil immersed himself in his studies and volunteering work, he felt a renewed sense of optimism about his future. He knew that the road ahead would be challenging, but he was determined to succeed.

With Vedant's advice guiding him, Swapnil focused on building his skills, expanding his network, and seizing every opportunity that came his way. He was determined to create a better life for himself and his family, just like Vedant had done.

Swapnil often confided about the challenges he faced in academics and volunteering work to Vedant, Vedant in return helped him out in myriad ways, by inspiring him, guiding him, and supporting him throughout. The friendship he found in Vedant was that of an elder brother, he seemed to know a lot about the world and helped Swapnil navigate new waters he was treading on.

As the days turned into weeks and the weeks into months, Swapnil remained steadfast in his resolve. He knew that success wasn't guaranteed, but he was willing to work hard and persevere. With each passing day, he moved one step closer to achieving his dreams. And as he looked towards the future, Swapnil felt a sense of excitement and anticipation for the journey ahead.

Chapter 10

The Door of Opportunity.

Swapnil indulged himself relentlessly in the volunteering duties of the social justice group, he anticipatingly awaited the weekends so he could get together with other fellow volunteers and create an impact in the community. He completely immersed himself in the tasks and duties assigned to him and began taking charge whenever it was required. His Sundays became dedicated to distributing food to the needy and organizing rallies for various causes.

In the process, he made new friends who shared his passion for making a difference in society. Among them was a friend who worked at the campus grocery store, both he and Swapnil gelled along quite well and stuck together whenever there were social justice group meetings. Both of them had a lot in common, especially when it came to their bigger ideas on humanity and service. Both of them wrapped up their assigned duties, and Swapnil's friend invited him to get food together. Swapnil hurriedly packed up his belongings in his bag as he made his way out, he politely declined his friend's invitation.

Unbeknownst to Swapnil, their conversation on this day would change his life's trajectory.

"I have to be somewhere, maybe some other time! I'll see you soon." He proclaimed as he was about to take his leave.

"Where do you disappear all day?" His friend asked, curious about Swapnil's whereabouts on Sundays. Every time he suggested hanging out after their volunteering work, Swapnil always came up with an excuse to leave.

Swapnil shrugged, "After college, I have my car washing job, so I have to go out for that."

His friend raised an eyebrow, "You're spending so much time on car washing. I work at the campus grocery store. Why don't you come there? I can talk to my manager for you." He declared.

Swapnil was skeptical. "I applied there before, but I didn't get the job." He was reminded of his initial days when he struggled with part-time job applications, especially within the university campus. Rejections poured in from all sides and he ultimately had to end up settling for the local car wash job as he was desperate for any gig that paid him enough to sustain himself.

His friend reassured him, "No, no, I have a good rapport with the manager. I'll get you in. Just give me your resume. You are hardworking; you'll definitely get opportunities."

Swapnil reluctantly handed over his resume, not expecting much to come of it. He went on with his routine as usual, slogging at the car wash job, finishing up household chores, attending lectures, and studying, however, this time he had his volunteering at the social justice group every weekend to look forward to.

A week passed and he had soon forgotten about his conversation with his friend. One day while he was on his way back home after attending a grueling lecture, he received a call from an unknown number. He looked at his phone trying to figure out who it could be, he did not recall handing out his number to anyone in particular in the past couple of weeks. But to his surprise, he received a call for an interview at the grocery store. The person on the side of the line gave him a date, venue, and time for the job interview. This job seemed like a dream compared to his current car washing job – it paid more, had fewer working hours, and was conveniently located on campus.

After ending the call Swapnil felt a rush of excitement, he gleamed in joy and trotted his way back to his apartment merrily, he was stoked to receive the call back from his job application. Owing to his past experience he was not expecting one. He messaged his friend thanking him for getting his application and resume across, his friend was happy for Swapnil and texted him back "Once you get the job, hopefully you won't bail on me anymore for grabbing food after work," Swapnil replied "Not at all!" Grinning from ear to ear. He started brainstorming on what to wear for the interview, he wanted to present the best version of himself. He prepped up his file, filled it with an updated resume and additional documents, and hoped for the best outcome.

The day of the interview came faster than expected, his nerves were beginning to get the best of him. "Calm down Swapnil, no point in getting all nervous now. I cannot afford to mess up this chance," he said to himself. He adjusted his collar and fixed his hair in front of the mirror before leaving the apartment with his file and bag.

While walking towards the interview location he felt grateful to even have the opportunity to attend the interview, "whatever happens, it'll be a learning lesson" he thought to himself.

He took a deep breath of air and opened the door. He saw a man sitting on a chair. Upon entry of Swapnil, the man greeted him, "You must be Swapnil?" Swapnil greeted him back politely, and responded "Yes I am, nice to meet you," he uttered as he made his way inside.

The man introduced himself as the manager of the store. Swapnil glanced around the store, making himself comfortable on the seat he was offered. The interview started off at ease, it felt informal almost. The manager seemed like an easy person to talk to.

During the interview, Swapnil felt a surge of confidence as he shared his experiences and aspirations with the manager. The manager seemed impressed, he pressed his glasses against his nose bridge firmly and said "We'll get back to you about our decision in two days, it was great meeting you Swapnil. Have a good day!"

"Sure, thank you for having me!" Swapnil smiled as he responded and took his leave.

On the way back he felt as though a huge weight had been lifted off his shoulder, the days leading up to the interview were anxiety-ridden, and he now felt he could breathe with ease. Unfortunately for him, that feeling did not last long, the moment he got home and lay on his bed, thoughts in his head began spiraling. He was now anxious about the results!

The two days that followed were agonizing for Swapnil. He couldn't sleep, constantly replaying the interview in his mind and hoping for a positive outcome. The prospect of a better job brought renewed hope and excitement, but it also intensified his anxiety.

As the hours ticked by on Monday, Swapnil's nerves were stretched to their limit. Every ring of his phone sent a jolt of anticipation through him, only to be followed by disappointment when it wasn't the call he was waiting for.

By 2:00 PM, Swapnil's patience was wearing thin. Just as he was about to give up hope, his phone finally rang, and it was the manager on the line, delivering the news he had been longing to hear – he got the job!

Swapnil's happiness knew no bounds. He couldn't believe his luck. He immediately shared the good news with his family and friends, his voice trembling with excitement as he recounted the journey from volunteering to securing the job. His parents wished him well before he began his new job, his father was proud of Swapnil for having come so far on his own. Swapnil thanked his friend from the social justice group, he messaged him saying "Our next meal together is one me, thank you for the opportunity. I owe you one big time!", his friend responded cheekily "Haha, looking forward to that! And congratulations Swapnil, it's all your work man."

Another person that Swapnil was immensely grateful for was Vedant, he believed he would not have been able to access this opportunity if he had not taken Vedant's advice a while ago.

Eager to share his joy with Vedant, Swapnil called him next. "You won't believe what happened to me!" He exclaimed, unable to contain his excitement.

"I got the job at the campus grocery store Vedant! Isn't that amazing? I finally don't have to slog at the car wash job, I'll have more time to myself and my studies now," he beamed with happiness. He shared the details of his journey with Vedant, expecting nothing but congratulations in return. However, Vedant's response took him by surprise.

There was a prolonged moment of stillness on the other side of the call. After what felt like a good minute or two, Vedant replied "I'm happy for you Swapnil, if this is what you wanted."

"Hmm, I feel like you are holding back on something, you don't seem very excited for me Vedant," Swapnil responded, sounding a little demotivated by Vedant's lackluster reply.

"Your life is set with just this? This is only the beginning. You've just opened the first door of opportunity. You need to aim higher," Vedant said.

Swapnil felt a mix of surprise and disappointment at Vedant's response. He felt a little gutted over the matter that one of his closest friends only had so much to say. It was supposed to be a happy moment for him, yet Vedant was already urging him to aim higher.

"Of course, I have bigger aspirations, but at this moment I consider landing the job quite a feat for me man, I'm disappointed that you don't see how big of a deal it is for me," a sombre Swapnil uttered.

Vedant sighed on the other end of the phone and spoke "Congratulations Swapnil, just forget about what I said, I realize it came across as too harsh."

Swapnil felt a range of mixed emotions, he wanted to justify his actions but held it within him. Still, he thanked Vedant for his advice and hung up, his mind buzzing with conflicting thoughts.

As Swapnil prepared for his new job, Vedant's words echoed in his mind. He felt a deep sense of gratitude for the opportunity that had come his way, but he also felt a newfound ambition stirring within him.

He contemplated on Vedant's advice, he understood where Vedant was coming from. He did realize that he might be aiming too low. He had huge aspirations but he did not lay down a plan and set a deadline to accomplish them, it felt as though his dreams were just phantom fractals lying around in his vast mind, they weren't a strong goalpost or anything of substance. They felt like fleeting clouds, drifting in different corners of his head.

He realized that getting a job at the grocery store was just the first step toward his goals. There were still many challenges to overcome and opportunities to seize. He resolved to work hard and strive for greater achievements in the future. He needed to have a firm plan to get to his goals, his mind wandered and so did his resolve from time to time. This time, after the call with Vedant, he felt like his spirit was reignited, he was hungry for more and was mentally prepared to go through and subdue any hindrance that was about to come in the way of him and his dreams.

As Swapnil stepped into his new role at the grocery store, he felt a sense of pride and determination. He knew that this job was just the beginning of his journey towards success. Looking out through the glass panes he was able to see the vast campus at its glory as the sun sank into the horizon. His new job was physically much easier on his body, and the lowered stress and fewer work hours benefited his academics greatly. He was back on good rapport with his lecturers, he made it a point to prioritize a good academic record above anything else. Every time his resolve faltered, Vedant's advice on the phone kept ringing in his ears. Something that had hurt him deeply that day had inadvertently turned into his biggest motivation now.

Armed with Vedant's advice and the support of his friends and family, Swapnil was ready to face whatever challenges lay ahead. He was determined to make the most of this opportunity and to continue striving for greatness in all aspects of his life.

All his friends along the way, Jaiveer, Armaan, and Vedant had a significant impact on his conscience and drive. He was glad to have friends that shaped him in a positive way for his highest good and betterment.

The journey from volunteering to securing a job at the grocery store had been filled with ups and downs, but it had ultimately led Swapnil to a brighter future. With each step forward, he gained valuable experiences and insights that would shape his path ahead. The invaluable lessons he learned along the way and the people he came across who managed to secure a cherished place in his heart all played a huge role in Swapnil becoming the man everyone knew him to be.

As Swapnil looked towards the future, he felt a sense of excitement and anticipation. He knew that there would be obstacles to overcome and challenges to face, but he was confident in his ability to succeed.

With his newfound job and a renewed sense of purpose, Swapnil was ready to embark on the next chapter of his life.

Chapter 11

The Path to Success

Fluorescent lights flickered above Swapnil as he glanced around the bustling aisles of the grocery store. The store had hundreds of people entering and exiting at different intervals, and shelves were updated and restocked daily. Swapnil saw many familiar and unknown faces navigating the isles, foraging through shelves looking for the product of their needs. A lot of the time, the tiny and peripheral system of the grocery store somehow felt akin to the larger system of a human's life, the sub-systems are a reflection of the larger systems that enclose them. People entered and exited Swapnil's life, same with success and failure, everything was constantly changing, just like how the grocery store never looked the same each time. The same building witnessed different changes in the stocks, the people, and the frequency of business with each day and changing seasons. Volatility is a sign of growth and transformation.

It had been over a year since he first stepped foot into the store, with an air of uncertainty and armed with determination. Now, as he scanned the rows of neatly stacked goods, he couldn't help but feel a sense of pride at how far he had come. A year changed rapidly, and so had his life.

Graduating from university had been a significant milestone in Swapnil's journey. It marked an important breakthrough in his life, where he had accomplished and fulfilled the quest to secure further education overseas. However, through his time in college, his dreams evolved with him, and his aim transformed into another quest of living the perfect life in Melbourne. This involved securing a visa for permanent residency and a job that would fulfill him. Despite the challenges he faced along the way, he managed to secure a decent position at the grocery store, earning a salary that allowed him to support himself and even send some money back home to his family. Yet, despite his achievements, a cloud of uncertainty loomed over him.

The impending expiration of his visa weighed heavily on Swapnil's mind. With the clock ticking and the passing of each moment, Swapnil felt a weight piling on his shoulders. To ease his worries he persistently tried to navigate what step to take next. He began by consulting various lawyers, each offering different advice and suggesting various pathways to secure his residency in Australia. From pursuing another course to moving to a remote area, the options seemed endless and overwhelming.

Feeling lost and unsure about what steps to take next, Swapnil found himself reaching out to an old friend he hadn't spoken to in months – Vedant. A wave of hesitation washed over him. Would Vedant be willing to help him again, especially after all this time?

“It has been a long time since we last spoke, I wonder if he'd mind talking to me,” he pondered, reminiscing on the good old times with Vedant.

Towards the end of his college, Vedant had turned into his confidante. He found solace in the company of someone who genuinely believed in him. Vedant was a dear friend who had inspired Swapnil magnanimously through living his own life in a dedicated, persistent way and also by telling Swapnil words that he needed to hear to propel him into fruitful conduct and actions. Swapnil opened his phone, scrolled through his contact list, and stopped at Vedant's name. He paused for a while and let out a feeble smile. He decided he would call him after all. If Vedant was anything like he remembered he would be the same old easy-to-talk to friend of Swapnil who always seemed to have it figured out.

As he dialed Vedant's number, he had a surge of nerves take over his body, however, it all disappeared when the familiar voice of Vedant on the other end of the line offered a sense of comfort and reassurance.

"Hello? Swapnil?" Vedant's voice echoed softly.

"Hello Vedant, how have you been? Hope it's a good time to talk?" Swapnil asked gently.

Swapnil heard a burst of joyous laughter from the other end of the phone, "wow you're being so formal! How have you been Swapnil? It's been a long time," he replied.

A significant time had passed since both of them had talked to each other, especially after their tense altercation which had occurred when Swapnil had shared the news of his new part-time job with Vedant. But it did not matter anymore, both of them went back to their fond memories with one another, a friendship that was meant to withstand the test of time and trouble.

Swapnil let out a huge grin and retorted, "I'm fine Vedant, so glad to be talking with you after such a long time. I miss hanging out with you man, we should catch up soon."

"Consider it done, but can I ask you something?" Vedant asked with a tone of concern, "Is everything fine from your side? I feel like you have something to tell me."

Swapnil sighed and replied, "I do, I have been conflicted and worried about a couple of important things actually."

"Go on," murmured Vedant.

With a deep breath, Swapnil began to pour out his troubles, sharing his fears and uncertainties about his visa situation and his future in Australia.

Vedant listened patiently, his calming presence offering solace to Swapnil's troubled mind. After Swapnil had finished speaking, Vedant offered his perspective, urging Swapnil not to dwell on the uncertainty of his visa status. Instead, he advised him to focus on whether his current job at the grocery store was related to his field of study. His advice deeply resonated with Swapnil, while the grocery store job had its perks, it was not aligned with Swapnil’s field of post-graduation. Swapnil decided to give Vedant’s advice some time to think about.

"Focus on doing your best in your current role," Vedant said reassuringly. "Everything else will fall into place eventually."

Swapnil felt a sense of relief wash over him as he absorbed Vedant's words of wisdom. For so long, he had been consumed by worry and doubt, but now, with Vedant's guidance, he felt a glimmer of hope flicker within him.

As the conversation came to an end, Swapnil couldn't help but feel grateful for Vedant's unwavering support and friendship. Despite the distance and time that had passed since they last spoke, Vedant had once again proven to be a pillar of strength in Swapnil's life.

With a renewed sense of determination, Swapnil hung up the phone, ready to face the challenges that lay ahead. Armed with Vedant's advice and the support of his friends and family, he knew that he would find a way to navigate the uncertainty and carve out a future for himself in Australia.

In the midst of uncertainty, Swapnil found solace in the wisdom of a friend. With Vedant's guidance, he embraced the challenges ahead with renewed hope and determination, knowing that he was not alone on this journey.

Hours turned into days and days turned into weeks, Swapnil began realizing the importance of what Vedant had told him and began looking for jobs that were within his area of expertise in terms of his post-graduation.

As Swapnil sat in his small apartment, the weight of uncertainty pressing down on his shoulders, he couldn't help but feel a sense of frustration. Despite Vedant's advice to focus on finding entry-level positions related to his education, Swapnil had spent countless hours scouring job boards and submitting applications, only to be met with silence in return. With each rejection letter that landed in his inbox, Swapnil's hopes dwindled, and the looming deadline of his visa expiration only added to his anxiety.

But amidst the sea of disappointment, a glimmer of hope emerged when Swapnil received an unexpected email one morning. It was an invitation to interview for a position that had become available at a local tech company due to another candidate backing out. Heart pounding with excitement, Swapnil quickly replied, accepting the invitation and scheduling the interview for the following week.

Swapnil eagerly began his preparation for the interview, he was keen on putting out the best of his skills and knowledge while also showcasing his capabilities as an individual. He even went out shopping to buy himself a fresh new set of formal clothing. Just like all the other interviews he had previously given, this one incited the same feelings of nervousness and flutters, however, Swapnil this time was a changed man, more confident, capable, and composed.

The morning of the interview, Swapnil woke up earlier than usual, made himself a warm mug of coffee, and sat on his couch, looking out through the window, gazing at the leaves of the trees rustling against one another. He took a sip out of the coffee mug and looked up, staring at his ceiling. He was curious about how the interview would unfold, he felt confident since he had a stacked resume with a decent amount of experience and exposure. After he took a quick shower, he got dressed in the new pair of clothes he had ironed the day before. He looked crisp and smart, ready to take the day by storm. He stepped out of his apartment and as he made his way towards the interview venue, a rush of gratitude washed over him. He was grateful for all the things falling in place right when he needed them to, he swiftly looked at his watch to make sure he was commuting as per the schedule. "Hope it all works out" he wondered.

As Swapnil entered the sleek office building on the day of the interview, nerves fluttering in his stomach, he couldn't help but marvel at how far he had come since his arrival in Australia. The journey had been filled with ups and downs, but in that moment, Swapnil felt a surge of determination coursing through his veins.

He entered the posh corporate meeting hall, the room was spick and span. The furnishing and interiors emitted an aura of sophistication. That, in sync with the high-end and contemporary embellishments, instilled a sense of awe in Swapnil. He looked at the panel of interviewers and approached them warmly. He greeted each one of them, firmly shook their hands, introduced himself briefly, and settled into the seat offered to him.

The interviewers looked like they could be anywhere between their thirties to fifties, they exuded an air of professionalism and experience. Swapnil was on his toes around the seasoned experts in front of him.

The interview room was engulfed in a pin-drop silence until one of the interviewers, looking through Swapnil's files looked up and asked him, "Hello Swapnil, are you ready to begin the interview?"

Swapnil looked at the interviewer with a face that emanated confidence and charisma. He replied, "Yes, I'm ready. Thank you for the opportunity!"

The interview itself passed by in a blur, with Swapnil drawing on his knowledge and experience to answer each question with confidence and poise. As he spoke passionately about his field of study and his eagerness to contribute to the company's success, Swapnil could sense a shift in the atmosphere, a palpable energy that seemed to resonate with the interviewers.

The interview was drawing closer to its conclusion. After the answer to the last question from the interviewers, one of the panel members looked at Swapnil with a smile and declared, "It was a pleasure interviewing you Swapnil, based on our conversation now, we'll be deciding if you are deemed fit for our organization."

Upon hearing the statement, Swapnil felt a sense of relief as well as looming anticipation. He sat on his chair as the panel of interviewers murmured incomprehensible words amongst each other. The air felt cold around him, it was starting to get daunting. After what felt like an eternity to Swapnil, one of the interviewers shared, "After significant consideration, all the panel members have come up with a final decision on your hiring process." Swapnil felt a lump in his throat, he was stumped for words, he did not expect the panel to reach to a decision immediately.

"We have decided to go forward with your application, we believe you are a suitable candidate for our company." The interviewer professed.

To his surprise and delight, the company offered Swapnil the job on the spot, impressed by his skills, dedication, and enthusiasm.

Swapnil felt a sensation of joy and gratitude take over every inch of his body, he was on the cloud nine!

"Thank you so much! I will make the best out of this amazing opportunity, thank you for taking the time to interview me," he proclaimed.

Overwhelmed with gratitude and relief, Swapnil accepted the offer, feeling a weight lift off his shoulders as he realized that his future in Australia was no longer hanging in the balance.

With the promise of employment came another glimmer of hope – the company assured Swapnil that they would handle his visa application, easing his worries about the impending deadline. This new information gave Swapnil immense hope, he thanked the interviewers again and shook their hands before parting ways. He walked towards the door with his documents in one hand, trying to subdue the staggering amount of emotions he was feeling.

Tears of joy welled up in Swapnil's eyes as he left the office, feeling a sense of pride and accomplishment wash over him.

That evening, as Swapnil sat in his apartment, reflecting on the whirlwind of emotions he had experienced that day, he felt compelled to reach out to the people who had supported him along the way. With trembling hands, he dialed his father's number, eager to share the good news and express his gratitude for all the sacrifices his family had made to support him in his journey.

As he listened to his father's joyful exclamations on the other end of the line, Swapnil couldn't help but feel a surge of gratitude for the unwavering love and support his family had shown him throughout his life. It was a moment of connection and shared joy that would stay with Swapnil forever, a reminder of the importance of family and the power of resilience in the face of adversity.

But there was one more person Swapnil felt compelled to thank – Vedant. With a sense of reverence, Swapnil composed a message to his friend, pouring his heart out in words of gratitude and appreciation. Vedant had been a guiding light in Swapnil's darkest moments, offering advice and encouragement that had ultimately led him to this moment of triumph.

To his surprise, Vedant's response was characteristically humble, downplaying his role in Swapnil's success and attributing it to Swapnil's own hard work and determination. But Swapnil knew better – without Vedant's guidance and support, he would never have had the courage to pursue his dreams and overcome the obstacles in his path.

Chapter 12

On the Greener Side

Three years later, Swapnil sat in his spacious office, a sense of contentment washing over him as he surveyed the bustling activity below. The years passed swiftly and smoothly to an extent, the journey was arduous, but it did amount to Swapnil living the dream that he had once dreamt of. He had come a long way since that fateful day of the interview, climbing the ranks within the company and earning the respect of his colleagues and superiors alike.

But perhaps even more rewarding than his professional success was the sense of fulfillment Swapnil felt in his personal life. With permanent residency secured and more time for his loved ones, Swapnil found himself enjoying the simple pleasures of life – spending time with family and friends, exploring new hobbies, and giving back to his community in meaningful ways.

As he scrolled through his social media feed one evening, Swapnil came across a message that caught his eye – a junior student from his alma mater in India expressing admiration for Swapnil's journey and sharing his own aspirations to study abroad. It was a poignant reminder of the ripple effect of inspiration and guidance, a testament to the power of sharing one's story and uplifting others along the way. Swapnil now reflected within himself to weather sell the dream of studying overseas to his junior like Jaiveer once did or should he give him the bitter reality check that he once would have needed himself. He thought to himself *Three years. Has it really been that long?* Swapnil thought as he leaned against the railing of his apartment balcony, staring out at the Melbourne skyline. The sun was setting, casting a golden hue over the city, and the gentle breeze carried with it the sounds of distant traffic and chatter from the streets below. The sight was breathtaking, but today, it brought a bittersweet smile to his face.

Swapnil is seated on his chair, overlooking the vast expanse of Melbourne's cityscape; the warm lighting in his office subdues the faint light coming from outside the glass panel. Swapnil rereads the message from the student, it reads;

"Dear Swapnil, I have been a follower of your socials for a long time now, I am from the same college as you! I find you inspiring and would love to take up the same venture of flying overseas for my further education. You have inspired me to dream beyond our finite imaginations. Looking at your life on my socials has ignited the fire in me to live a fascinating and wonderful life myself! Hope you read my message, have a good day."

The message baffles me, I can't come up with an appropriate response to the student's message. Should I thank him and encourage him, or give him a gist of what it takes to get here?

The dream that was sold to me? Or the unbridled reality that unfolded as soon as I stepped foot here?

Three years since I landed here with nothing but a suitcase, a heart full of hope, and a head full of dreams.

Back then, the idea of studying overseas felt like stepping into a new world—a world where everything would be better and easier. Whenever I saw Jaiveer's social media posts, it incited the same feeling the student was probably feeling looking at my profile. My parent's support and sacrifice were immeasurable, it took a lot just to step foot in another country, let alone begin a life there. I remember the day I first arrived in Australia as an international student from India. The air felt different, the people were different, and everything seemed... bigger. I had a feeling things were going to take a huge turn from the moment I sat on the flight to Melbourne, I just did not know how it would unfold. I had spent months preparing for that moment, and the excitement was palpable. Safe to say, it had been quite the ride, from the first day that I landed in Australia.

I thought it would all be smooth sailing. Get my degree, find a job, and live the dream. That's what everyone back home thinks, isn't it? But reality… He chuckled softly, shaking his head. *Reality has a way of pulling the rug out from under you.*

The truth was, the journey had been anything but smooth. It had been rough, exhausting, and at times, even soul-crushing. From the initial hurdles of the final step of my admission to securing a part-time job to get by, I had spent nights questioning my decisions, wondering if I had made a huge mistake. The loneliness hit hard, especially in the beginning. And nothing feels more miserable than having to deal with an injury or poor physical health when you don't have anyone you can rely on, that's when the depth of loneliness starts setting in. The time I had sprained my ankle was a true test of my persistence and will, had it not been for my family and my aspirations, it would have been the straw that broke the camel's back. I missed the familiar sights and sounds of Delhi—the bustling streets, the aroma of street food, the warmth of my family. Home can never be replaced by any place far and wide, it could be the safest, coziest of places or the most glorious of views, the true comfort and intimacy lie amongst familiarity and close bonds. And here, in this foreign land, I was just another face in the crowd, struggling to find my place.

No one talks about that, do they? The isolation, the homesickness, the sheer weight of being alone in a new country. Swapnil sighed. *Everyone back home only sees the highlights—the beautiful pictures, the stories of success. But they don't see the sleepless nights, the constant pressure to succeed, the fear of failure.*

I remember the first time I failed an assignment. Back in India, I had always been a top student, confident in my abilities, I made it to the top of my class almost every time, and I was pumped to show my new university my capabilities. But here, the academic system was different and more demanding. It wasn't just about knowing the material but also about critical thinking, something I wasn't used to. That first failure shook me to my core. I was thousands of miles away from home, with no one to turn to. I did not know how to deal with setbacks, because all that was known to me was academic success. I just dealt with them as they came, learning on the way, from others and the voice inside my heart. It was still hard, it was a tremendous shift, culturally, mentally, and physically. By the end of each day, I was drained beyond help. Sometimes I wished I could run away from all of it, and stay in the comfort of my home and the warm embrace of my family, my deepest, darkest thoughts kept emerging whenever I was faced with hardships initially.

But you can't let them see you struggle. You can't tell them how hard it really is. He'd learned to keep his struggles to himself, to put on a brave face for the folks back home. After all, he didn't want to worry them. *They had sacrificed so much for me to be here. How could I let them down?*

I pushed myself harder and took on part-time jobs to make ends meet. Even after I did end up finding my first part-time job, it was daunting. By the end of the car wash job hours, every bit of my arms, back and legs ached, the next day morning I was stiff with soreness. I wondered how I pushed through and made it to class without succumbing to the lure of my cozy bed. Slowly but surely, I did find my footing. Especially when I found an ideal job at my campus grocery store. But the challenges didn't stop there. The job market was ruthless. I had applied to countless positions and faced rejection after rejection, and each time, it chipped away at my confidence. Had I not dealt with failures, I might not have been here, maybe it was a rite of passage, an unavoidable sign of growth and maturity that has helped me immensely. Days passed and I remained hopeless, I had started to give in to my circumstances and accept whatever I was going through.

Everyone thinks that once you graduate, jobs will come pouring in. But they don't realize how competitive it is, how much harder you have to work just to get noticed.

Eventually, I did land a job, a great one at that, I feel fulfilled after an arduous ordeal of job hunting and securing a visa, and now, three years later, I am a permanent resident. Some days I like to think of it as luck, because I know many hardworking individuals who weren't able to secure a visa and had to pack their bags and leave for home, and on other days I like to think I have achieved all these feats through sheer hard work, persistence, and quick thinking. Either could be true and I would still be happy with the outcome that bore me. On paper, I have achieved what I had set out to do. But the journey left me scarred in ways I had not anticipated. I did not expect the outcome would have numerous hurdles on its path, it is all made it look nice and easy, no? But that was not how it felt for me, and probably several others too. There are days when I look back and wonder, if I had not taken the big leap of moving overseas several years ago, what life would I be living right now?

Would I do it all over again if I knew how hard it would be? He pondered the question, but deep down, he knew the answer.

I am definitely and wholeheartedly grateful for the opportunities I have come across here, but, just sometimes I wished someone had told me the truth from the beginning. The truth about how hard things would turn out to be. It was not the smoothest of rides or even the smoothest of roads, but it did amount to something at the end. However, I also know that people like Armaan might think otherwise, there is a good amount of privilege with which I speak, but I also know that things were not completely easy for me. It took a lot for the results and the fruits of labour to ripen, maybe if I would have had a better chance of coming in prepared for the long days if I had more guidance, it would have helped me ease into a totally new life well equipped. A little word of caution and tell perhaps, would have lent some assistance. There is, nevertheless, no doubt that I would still choose to come overseas after knowing the grim reality.

The dream to study overseas is alluring, but it's not the fairy tale everyone imagines. It's hard. It's lonely. And it can break you if you're not prepared. I wish I could tell every aspiring student back home to see the dream with caution, to understand the reality before making the leap.

I think if a student were to understand how the world overseas works, especially as a foreign student looking to settle abroad, one would tread the waters much more cautiously. The reality portrayed is often not nuanced and quite honestly, a facade. It takes an insurmountable amount of grit and determination to fly high and succeed in a completely new environment when no one seems to be looking out for you. However, there is a fair share of joy, learning, and gratitude in this journey. The friends you make along the way when you are going through some of your worst times are the friendships that will last you a lifetime. I am grateful to have come across some of the most hardworking, kind, and genuine people on my path towards my dream life. Jaiveer, a childhood friend and one of the few people who inspired me to take up the venture of moving overseas. Armaan, who showed what human grit and persistence are capable of, and his remaining true to himself and spreading positivity in times of adversity taught me that, life is not what happens to you, it is how you react to it. Vedant almost felt like a godsent figure, he taught me to stay put on my path and think smartly and rationally, leveraging all the opportunities that came my way. It is the happy memories and bonds you make along the way that make it all feel like it was worth it in the end.

Maybe that is what I need to do—share my story, the real story, so others know what they're getting into.

The sun had dipped below the horizon now, and the city lights began to twinkle like stars in the distance. Swapnil took a deep breath, feeling a sense of resolve settle within him. *It's time to stop pretending that everything was easy. It's time to tell the truth.*

And as Swapnil reflected on his own journey – the challenges overcome, the lessons learned, and the moments of triumph – he couldn't help but feel a sense of gratitude for the people who had walked beside him every step of the way. From his family and friends to mentors like Vedant, each person had played a vital role in shaping his path to success, reminding him that no dream is too big and no obstacle too insurmountable when faced with courage, determination, and unwavering faith in oneself.

The light of dawn, sets in after the darkness of the dusk.

In the journey of life, Swapnil found that success is not just about reaching the destination, but about embracing the challenges along the way and finding strength in the support of those who believe in you. As he looked back on his own journey, Swapnil realized that every setback, every obstacle, had ultimately led him to where he was meant to be – a place of fulfilment, purpose, and endless possibility. And as he embraced the future with open arms, Swapnil knew that the best was yet to come.

Conclusion

Swapnil's story echoes the voice of thousands of unheard students who go through tremendous challenges while pursuing an education overseas. The chronicles simulate what it would be like to traverse across a new land, finding one's voice, purpose, and identity. Our homeland often takes up a huge share of our identity, but when that is parted from us, it becomes a challenge to navigate the world outside and within oneself in an unknown territory.

Through a series of incidents and happenings that are inspired by real-life circumstances, a student aspiring to move abroad for education can get a panoramic idea of what it is like to live the dream of many. Many a time, we are frequently exposed to the dreamy and success stories of those who make it big, however, many individuals like Armaan are left in the dust. The other characters in the book represent different archetypes of the students who take up the feat of fulfilling their dreams overseas.

Beyond self-exploration and growth, there also lies succeeding in a foreign land. Because of the vast number of students with diverse ethnicities, aptitudes, and education, it tends to get highly competitive and hard to leave a mark. The journey of moving overseas should be seen as an all-encompassing experience that adds value to us by expanding our horizons, mentally and through varied opportunities, instead of trying to lead a picture-perfect life filled with no flaws.

The ordeals of Swapnil and his friends are examples based on real-life cases that happen quite frequently to international students. The feat might seem impressive, but it might be a very personal and individual experience that cannot be clubbed into a generalized experience. Opinions from those around us and those who have been overseas or stay overseas are always meant to be taken with a grain of salt; after all, no one likes to bite the hand that feeds you!

For countless Indian students, studying abroad represents the pinnacle of ambition, an opportunity to transform dreams into reality. The allure of global exposure, superior education, and the promise of better career prospects fuel these aspirations. From a young age, many are imbued with the belief that an international education is the key to unlocking a successful future, laden with prosperity and prestige. However, the reality that awaits these students abroad often stands in enormous contrast to their initial expectations, revealing a path riddled with challenges that test their resilience, adaptability, and determination.

Before embarking on their journey, Indian students often envision a life of academic rigor complemented by cultural exploration. The anticipation of studying in a foreign country brings with it images of state-of-the-art campuses, diverse student communities, and a lifestyle filled with both intellectual and social enrichment. They imagine themselves becoming part of a global network, gaining knowledge that not only enhances their expertise but also broadens their worldview. The promise of internships and job opportunities in international markets further fuels their optimism, as they envision themselves seamlessly transitioning into roles in top companies, earning in foreign currencies, and building a life that would make their families proud.

However, once these students arrive in their host countries, the reality often diverges sharply from their expectations. One of the first challenges they encounter is the cultural shock. Despite being exposed to Western culture through media, the lived experience of it can be overwhelming. The sense of alienation that comes with being in a foreign land, where everything from language to social norms differs from what they have known, can be daunting. Simple daily interactions can become sources of stress, and the feeling of being an outsider can lead to a deep sense of loneliness. Instances of prejudice occur quite frequently, especially in places they might not be exposed to individuals of different cultures or ethnicities.

Moreover, the academic pressure in international institutions can be significantly higher than what students are accustomed to. The emphasis on independent research, critical thinking, and class participation can be a steep learning curve for those used to a more didactic style of education. This academic culture shock is compounded by the challenge of balancing studies with part-time work, which many students take up to manage the high cost of living and tuition fees. The Indian culture, quite contrary to those abroad, often emphasizes on students depending on their parents financially until they secure a job, it is in contrast to the culture overseas that promotes autonomy over familial dependence. The financial burden can become a significant source of anxiety, as students grapple with the pressure to excel academically while also working to make ends meet.

The social challenges are equally formidable. Building friendships in a foreign country can be difficult, especially in environments where social circles are already established, and language barriers persist. The initial excitement of being in a new country often gives way to homesickness and a longing for the familiarity of home. The support systems that students rely on back home, such as family and friends, are no longer immediately accessible, making it harder to cope with the emotional and mental stress that accompanies this transition. It quite literally becomes, to each, their own. It is important to be prepared to deal with issues that might come in between socializing and forming genuine friendships.

The financial challenges faced by Indian international students are among the most significant hurdles in their journey abroad. Tuition fees for international students are often exorbitant, and the cost of living in foreign countries, especially in Western nations, can be prohibitively high. Many students rely on loans to fund their education, creating a heavy financial burden that looms over them throughout their studies. To alleviate some of this pressure, students often take up part-time jobs. However, balancing these jobs with academic responsibilities is no easy feat. The demands of work can detract from study time, leading to a cycle of stress and burnout. Furthermore, the exchange rate fluctuations can exacerbate financial strain, as the value of the Indian rupee against stronger currencies can result in increased financial obligations for students and their families back home.

The mental health challenges arising from these financial pressures are profound. Constant worry about finances can lead to anxiety and depression, especially when coupled with the academic stress and cultural isolation students often face. The stigma surrounding mental health issues in Indian society can make it difficult for students to seek help, leaving them to struggle in silence. The lack of familiar support systems in a foreign country further compounds this issue, leading to feelings of loneliness and despair. In extreme cases, this combination of financial and mental health stressors can lead to severe consequences, such as dropping out of school or even contemplating self-harm. It is essential to have a healthy relationship with oneself mentally, and seek help if the need ever arises. A healthy mind births genius ideas and a holistic life.

The gap between the dream and reality of studying abroad thus extends beyond the academic and cultural challenges—it also encompasses the financial strain and the toll it takes on mental health. Addressing these issues requires more than just individual resilience; it calls for greater awareness, better support systems, and accessible resources to help students navigate these difficult circumstances.

To end on a holistic note, while the dream of studying abroad is often seen through rose-tinted glasses, the reality presents a more complex picture. The journey of an Indian international student is one of immense growth and learning, but it is also fraught with challenges that test their perseverance. The experience of studying abroad, while valuable, demands more than just academic preparedness—it requires emotional resilience, cultural adaptability, and the ability to navigate the uncertainties that come with stepping into a world vastly different from one's own. Ultimately, the gap between the dreams of studying abroad and the reality is not a deterrent but a crucible through which students emerge stronger, more independent, and better equipped for the globalized world they sought to be part of.

The decision to take up the venture of moving should be a carefully decided endeavor, entailing thorough research, proper planning, and extensive support. It is an exciting and thrilling venture that should be considered with extensive input. Ultimately, the decision depends on personal goals, financial considerations, and long-term aspirations.

Riddled with raw truths and stories of perseverance, the book acts as a blueprint for the everlasting and massive overtaking of 'Dreaming Overseas'.